A LORD EDGINGTON INVESTIGATES
NOVELLA

A
N°VEL
WAY T° KILL

A 1920s   MYSTERY

D1513764

BENEDICT BROWN

COPYRIGHT

For my father, Kevin,
I hope you would have liked this book an awful lot.

READER'S NOTE

I wrote this book as a spoiler-free introduction to my 1920s detective series "Lord Edgington Investigates…" It stands alone as a story in its own right, with no hint of any longer plot arcs or spoilers for any of the other mysteries.

It is actually the ninth book in the series, coming between "The Crimes of Clearwell Castle" and "The Snows of Weston Moor" but if you haven't read the books that came before, you can still jump into this one without any trouble.

I hope you absolutely love it!

CHAPTER ONE

"So tell me, dear boy, are you ready for your first lesson?"

There were two things that bothered me that day. First, my grandfather, the renowned sleuth, Lord Edgington, had woken me at the perfectly uncivilised hour of nine in the morning to drag me out to the rose garden of his palatial property. And second, after a year and a half spent solving crimes together, he only now believed that my training to become a detective had begun.

Still, I did not have to consider his question for long. "I've never been more prepared for anything in my life." It was at this moment that he pulled a gun from his pocket, and I quickly changed my mind. "Then again, I heard it might rain this morning. Perhaps we should return to the house."

He dismissed my protest with a shake of the head. "Christopher, having thought very carefully about your training, I've decided that we should start with a bang." The old chap let out a cackle, and the white whiskers above his lips stretched out as though he'd received an electric shock.

"What are you doing with that?" I found the courage to point one finger in the direction of the savage pistol, though, in all honesty, I would rather have hidden behind the nearest rose bush with my fingers in my ears. Our golden retriever Delilah did just that – except for the fingers part – and wouldn't be seen for some time.

"Really, boy, there's nothing to fear. I am merely going to teach you how to—"

I would never get to discover exactly what he had planned for me, as it was at this moment that my saviour arrived.

"I'm sorry to interrupt, M'Lord." Our full-time chauffeur, part-time butler and all-round good egg, Todd, was carrying a small tray with a neat white envelope laid upon it. He must have come from the house in a hurry as he was wearing his butler's waistcoat and driving cap. Realising his mistake, he swiped the hat from his head and hid it behind his back as he bowed to present the missive.

"Urgent," I read aloud, as it is my job to observe the most starkly apparent facts.

Todd straightened up once more and offered a further apology. "I wouldn't have bothered you, M'Lord, but the messenger was insistent that you should receive it as soon as possible."

"It has a Suffolk postmark," Grandfather revealed a little more insightfully. Even such minor deductions impressed me.

I took a step closer to examine the envelope. "Who do you imagine could have sent it?"

He held it up to the light of the pale autumn sun, which hovered in the sky not so very high above us. "There is one method for discovering that very thing."

"Gosh! Do you mean to say that you know a special technique for—" I began, before identifying a hint of amusement in his gaze and responding accordingly. "You're implying we should open it. Aren't you, Grandfather?"

He smiled and did just that. "You're already learning, Chrissy. Scotland Yard will come begging for your assistance in no time." He extracted a stiff rectangular card from its envelope and stood mumbling to himself. "Interesting. Very interesting."

Todd came to stand on the other side of him and we both waited to discover what news the letter contained.

"Extremely interesting!" he continued, and I was about to prompt him to share the details with his two most loyal companions when he did just that. "It's an invitation from the Shipley Sisters."

"Well, that is interesting!" Todd exclaimed, and I was tempted to pretend I knew to whom they were referring, but... well... I hadn't a clue.

"I've never heard of them."

The two men looked appalled by my ignorance.

"Nessa Shipley?" Todd practically poked me with these words.

"And her sisters, Eve and Livia?" Grandfather contributed. "You must have heard of the Shipley sisters. They're greatly admired by all the most respected names in their field."

I was trying to imagine exactly where that field might be located when my grandfather put me out of my misery. "They're writers, Christopher. Nessa is known for her history of the Queens of England. Eve has travelled the world and written about half of it, and as for Livia—"

"She's a mystery writer!" Todd could not hold in his excitement any longer. "I read her book 'The Seven Sisters of Solomon Leroux' last year. It was so good that I immediately devoured everything else she'd written. She creates quite the most puzzling murders I've come across."

Though a marquis, and the owner of one of the largest estates in the southeast of England, Grandfather was not one of those stuffy lords who refused to allow his staff to act like normal human beings and expected reverence at all times. And yet, even he looked at his chauffeur a little perplexedly as the man waxed lyrical on his literary heroine.

"She's a genius, an absolute genius. You simply must read her books." With this final entreaty issued, Todd clasped his mouth firmly shut.

"I have heard that Livia Shipley is a capable writer of *popular fiction.*" Grandfather pronounced this expression as though it was some kind of insult. "But these mystery novels with which young people today are so enamoured have very little of substance in them. I believe that her older sister's efforts are more impressive. Having read her fascinating work on the English Civil War, it is Nessa Shipley that I am most eager to meet."

"So we're going to Suffolk?" Both Todd and I enquired with expert synchronism as though we'd been practising this moment for months.

Grandfather did not look quite as excited as we were but nodded all the same. "That's correct. We have been invited to dinner this evening at their estate near Southwold on the east coast. Pearson House is an ancient property and I have long wanted to—" He cut himself short as it was clear that we weren't particularly interested in the history of the building and only wished to cross paths with a famous detective novelist.

Todd and I chattered away about this very topic all the way back to the house. The golden-cream towers of Cranley Hall seemed to shimmer in the morning light. Not that I had time to marvel at the place just then. I had a bag to pack and breakfast to eat. Though a fine detective, an excellent mentor, and one of Scotland Yard's most celebrated former officers, my grandfather had a habit of forgetting that I was a growing boy who required at least five square meals a day. Very well, four at a push, but I hadn't got to eighteen years of age by starving myself!

Once I had eaten two bacon and egg sandwiches, consumed a large helping of orange juice and polished it all off with a healthy selection of cakes, I managed to walk out to the front of the property. Delilah was busy circling the car with her tail wagging and would occasionally mount the running board to await her master.

She wasn't the only one who was excited by the possibility of one of my grandfather's impromptu voyages through the English countryside, though. By the time we were ready to leave, a large group had amassed. Amidst a crowd of household staff and gardeners, our ageing footman, Halfpenny, had an optimistic smile on his face, the fearsome maid, Dorie, was humming inanely to herself – so nothing new there – and our beloved cook, Henrietta, had left her kitchen with high hopes of a place aboard the Rolls Royce Phantom, which Todd had prepared for the journey.

"Good morning, M'Lord," she said with a blush on her skinny cheeks.

"Good morning, Henrietta," Lord Edgington replied with a respectful half-bow. He was fonder of his employee and her eccentric culinary creations than anyone I knew. He rarely travelled without her, which is why she was looking quite so expectant.

"Will you be needing my services today, M'Lord?"

He climbed into the back of the vehicle before responding. It was always a relief when he decided not to drive himself and allowed the professional to do his job.

"Not today, I'm afraid."

Cook struggled at first but eventually landed upon a response. "But… but you hate to rely on the food of other families' cooks. You've told me yourself on any number of occasions."

He turned his head to one side as though considering this unique dilemma. "That is true, but we're only going for one night. I can hardly impose my tastes upon a stranger's dinner party now, can I?"

"No, M'Lord." The poor woman was close to tears. "Of course not, M'Lord."

A disappointed pallor fell across the faces of our most regular travelling companions as they came to accept that they would also be staying at home for the weekend. Some might have described such a reaction – and the fact that Halfpenny had already packed a bag – as presumptuous, but it was Grandfather's fault for insisting on taking half the population of Cranley with him wherever we went. To give him his due, he did look sorry as those employees who were surplus to requirements morosely returned to their tasks.

Of course, his guilt did not last long. Once everyone had left, he smiled broadly and gave his instructions to his driver. "Off we go, Todd. Suffolk awaits!"

CHAPTER TWO

It had only been a few months since my grandfather and I had returned from a long (slightly body-strewn) tour of South West England, and now we were setting off once more. I'd been twiddling my thumbs at Cranley Hall, and it felt sublime to be back on the road again.

The trees that lined the dappled lanes of Surrey had grown tired of their summer wardrobes. The once lush greenery had been replaced with a new kaleidoscope of colours, with everything from golden brown to sunset red on display in the leaves that waved to us as the Rolls glided down the tarmac at great speed. It wasn't just the pace at which my grandfather normally drove that scared me. Todd seemed to have an innate knowledge of whichever vehicle he drove, so that even the speediest journey was as smooth as an ocean cruise whenever he was at the helm.

"It's rather interesting that we should receive this invitation so late, don't you think, Christopher?"

"Yes, interesting," I replied, as this was evidently the word of the day.

"Like all the great literary families, the sisters have a reputation for eccentricity, but I wonder why they only sent the message on the day of the event."

"Perhaps someone else cancelled, and you were the second choice," I said without thinking, and the wise old chap took exception to the idea.

"I very much doubt that would be the case." He folded his arms across his chest and looked out through the window at the muddy fields where, but one month earlier, high stalks of wheat had stood proud. "Perhaps they need my expert opinion on something. Perhaps they fear a crime is about to take place." It was his turn to sound enthusiastic on a topic, though I had a bucket of water to pour on these suggestions.

"Far be it from me to suggest that we will not be required to investigate some terrible crime this weekend (as that does seem to happen wherever we go)," I didn't actually say these last nine words, but I was definitely thinking them. "But it seems unlikely that they'd invite us to dinner if what they really needed was a detective to solve a crime."

"Well…" he began, and when that didn't work, he tried, "But…." That wasn't the ticket either and, after a brief, "You know…" he gave up and fell silent.

We travelled through the bucolic county of Surrey before entering the sprawling metropolis of London and crossing the Thames at Tower Bridge. We even stopped for a spot of lunch at the Ritz! I knew the journey well as, only the summer before, we'd followed that exact route to visit a former friend, lover and rival of my enigmatic forebear's.

"Yes, I had considered the possibility that the letter would be from a member of the Rous family." Grandfather had a habit of reading my mind, and I didn't like it one bit. He was not, in fact, a clairvoyant but merely an experienced interpreter of body language. I was struggling to work out exactly which twitch or expression could have revealed what I'd been thinking when he continued. "I recently heard that the Earl of Stradbroke is on his last legs, and I was rather relieved when the note did not contain bad news."

"Jolly good!" I said, as how else is a boy to reply to such a statement?

After our meagre feast, we travelled north, plunging back into the countryside on our way towards Ipswich and beyond. It was nice to take the more comfortable A-roads for once. My grandfather's love of adventure often led us down unbeaten tracks, and I must say that a gliding voyage was far preferable to a jolting one.

Nearly at our destination, we passed Henham Park, where Lord Edgington had spent many summers in his youth. It was ringed by a thick forest, and we could see nothing of the manor house within, but it was no surprise that we would not be stopping there for tea. I had once struggled to accept the idea that my grandfather could be anything less than everyone's favourite person, but the knowledge was well-lodged in my brain by this point.

And then, before I knew it, Todd was pulling off the road onto a long, gravel drive that led us to a rambling mansion. I must have seen a hundred country houses in my time, and yet each new pile we visited offered something different. With its Flemish gables, white sash windows as far as the eye could see and red-brick façade, it was presumably Stuart in design, though it had any number of more modern touches that could only have been added by the know-it-all Victorians. A new wing had been tacked onto one side and there were twisting chimneys popping up all over, arranged in symmetrical groupings across the roof.

As the Rolls came to a halt on the gravel drive, I was rather eager to discover what eccentric mishmash lay behind the charming exterior. Before dear Delilah and I could jump from the vehicle, the front door opened, and three women emerged from the house with smiles on their faces and matching waddles. Arranged by height, they were like a line of ducks crossing a busy road. It was hard to estimate their age as they looked both terribly old and brightly innocent, but when the first of them spoke, I decided that they couldn't be younger than sixty if they were a day.

"Lord Edgington, my name is Nessa Shipley. It's so good of you to come," the first in line boomed over to us. She had a distinctly plummy voice, as though practising a script for the London stage.

"So good of you," the subsequent Shipley sisters intoned.

They came to a stop a few feet from the car and fanned out like an army defending a military line.

"It's so good of you to invite us," Grandfather's voice was a little less certain than I would have expected, and I noticed that even he couldn't resist echoing their words. "And you mustn't worry yourselves about the lateness of the invitation. I was happy to drop what I was doing for the chance to visit your famous property." He paused to marvel at the impressive building, as Todd drove off around the stone island in front of the house and parked the Phantom in the shadow of a monkey puzzle tree.

"We would have invited you earlier," the first woman began. "Except—"

The shorter of her two sisters interrupted before she could get the words out. "Except we didn't know until last night that our original guest had cancelled." She had a blunter tone than the other two and looked a shrewd character. I was jumping to conclusions, of course, but I had to assume she was the famous mystery novelist (of whom I had never heard until that day). "I was looking forward to hearing old Captain Hardjack's tales of the sea. But beggars can't be choosers, and you'll have to do."

As Grandfather wrinkled his nose up at this slight slight, I examined the three women more carefully. The historian, Nessa Shipley, had a wide, earnest face, which she decorated with a pleasant smile. She was every part the good host and won some real points with me for immediately kneeling to receive affection from our ever-so-loving canine. Delilah even licked the lady's face, and Nessa didn't flinch.

The woman in the middle presented the oddest picture of the three. She had unruly white hair and bushy eyebrows, and her dress was visibly draggle-tailed, as though she'd spent the afternoon parading through puddles. The gown itself was a pale pink, which was clearly not the original colour, and I could only imagine it had changed in the wash. Though she was a messy sight in contrast to her more formally attired siblings, I found her chaotic presence rather endearing. In fact, it was only the petite third sister to whom I took exception.

She stared at me as though I were an inconvenience – which, admittedly, I often was. She narrowed her eyes, perhaps trying to make sense of what some upstart adolescent was doing at the great detective's side. In the end, her gaze was so forceful that I found myself answering her unspoken question.

"My name's Christopher," I said, stumbling over this simple sentence so that I sounded quite the dunce. "The grandson."

Grandfather gave me a sharp glare of his own just then, and I knew exactly what he meant.

"Full sentences, please, Christopher," I unwittingly blurted on his behalf, and then did as I had instructed. "I'm Lord Edgington's grandson. I help him with his cases from time to time… Well, *help* is rather a strong word. I'm more likely to—"

I cut this comment short, as Grandfather's expression had changed. It now said, *You're rambling, Christopher. Please don't.*

"It's a pleasure to be here," he said aloud and then confirmed the identities of our hosts so that they didn't have to. "Nessa, Livia and Eve." He nodded to each one, and it turned out I was mistaken in my assumption. The mystery novelist was not the short, suspicious character, but the sweet, purblind simpleton with the vagabond appearance. And that is a rather perfect indication of my limited talents as a detective.

"Please, come this way." Eagle-eyed Eve waved her hand and led the parade inside. "I imagine you would like a tour of the house." She did not wait for an answer but began the most detailed description of a property I had ever endured.

"Pearson House was, in fact, built for the Staplehurst family in 1682, though it would not be used by them until a century later, due to financial constraints. In the meantime, Admiral Hercules Adnams occupied the place on a fifty-year lease which was renewed on the thirteenth of April 1743 – the very same day that the British East India Company's ship, Princess Louisa, was wrecked off the Sotavento island of Maio. Forty-nine souls were lost of the one hundred and seventy-nine crew on board."

We'd only made it into the cramped entrance hall, where a painting of the Admiral was on display, and I couldn't resist a query. "I'm sorry, but was Admiral Adnams somehow connected to the shipwreck?"

Eve rolled her eyes. "No, of course he wasn't, boy. It was merely a coincidence. And I would appreciate it if you could leave all questions until the end."

"Eve, dear," her elder (or at least taller) sister responded. "Please be polite to our guests."

"Yes, yes." The youngest sister tutted a little before taking us into the main reception room which gave onto various larger spaces. It was far grander than the naval-themed porch we had passed through and was rather dominated by a gigantic crystal chandelier that hung high on the ceiling. "Now, the two Chinese vases you can see at the entrance to the drawing room are, in fact, not Chinese at all…"

This was how our introduction to Pearson House began and continued and, indeed, seemed to go on for some hours. It was hard to imagine that, of the three sisters, Eve was the travel writer, not the historian. She appeared to know everything there was to about the centuries during which the building had been standing. If anything, she knew too much, and I was soon yawning. Perhaps it was due to the mild weather or the fact there were no windows open, but I was afraid I might fall asleep standing up.

The house itself was beautiful, and I did enjoy the chance to examine so many of its magnificent rooms but, at the point at which she led us into the snug, having already visited a small study, the downstairs cloakroom and several of the bathrooms, I did have to wonder whether such an exhaustive presentation was entirely necessary.

"And this," she said with some finality when we got to the top of the house, "is Daddy's room."

She opened the door for the pair of us to troop inside – Delilah having sensibly lain down in one of the salons on the ground floor and forsaken the rest of the tour. It was a simple bedroom with a nightstand, brocade curtains and, to my surprise, an old man lying in bed, snoring away to himself.

"Don't worry," Nessa said quite loudly. "He's a heavy sleeper and practically deaf. He won't hear a thing."

I felt rather rude to be invading the poor fellow's personal boudoir, but Eve continued straight on with the final chapter of the house's history. "A man named Martin once died in this room, though you needn't worry about his ghost coming to haunt you. For some reason he hasn't yet explained, he is only ever seen in the attic, which can only be reached during the summer."

The three of them were clearly lunatics and, though I would like to have known a little more about Martin the ghost – and how a room could only be accessed one season out of four – I held my tongue and was most relieved when the time came to traipse back downstairs.

CHAPTER THREE

Grandfather had prepared a special treat for our hosts and had our chauffeur and part-time barman pop by with his portable case of bottles and special glasses, to mix us a cocktail before dinner.

"It's known as a Sazerac," Todd explained as he proceeded to rinse several glasses out with absinthe before drowning a sugar cube in cognac and adding a dash of bitters. "It comes all the way from New Orleans and is one of the oldest American cocktails. I believe it's been making a stir in Paris this year."

The sisters nodded politely, clearly impressed by the strapping chap's technique. The only problem came when I counted the glasses and realised he'd mixed one for me, too. To be perfectly honest, I couldn't understand the fuss that adults made over alcohol. I found orange juice or a nice glass of lemonade far more refreshing.

"Thank you, Todd," I said as he bowed and retreated from the room with his case.

I turned my glass around a few times in the hope it might make the noxious substance easier to drink. Grandfather and the three sisters were sipping at the amber liquid like a cup of tea, and I raised it to my nose. The smell nearly knocked me out, so it was lucky I never had to drink any.

"Christopher," my grandfather began. "would you perhaps prefer a glass of water?"

Looking quite amused at the display, our hosts got to enjoy the full range of my grimaces before I recovered enough to reply.

"Yes, please, Grandfather," I said before he could take back the offer.

He kindly poured me my much safer drink, then cleared his throat and looked for something to discuss before dinner. "That was a fascinating tour, thank you, ladies. But there was one thing that was not explained."

I find that hard to believe! I considered interrupting, though it would only have led to more disdainful glances from Eve.

"If the original owners of your beautiful abode were the Staplehursts, why was the property christened Pearson House?"

The three looked at one another from the other side of the long table. "You know that's a jolly good question," Nessa replied with her usual cheerful energy.

"Nobody knows," Eve crossed her arms across her chest as though put out. "The three of us have done what we can to discover the truth, but there's simply no record of any connection to a Pearson."

"The cat!" Livia put in. "I still say it was named after the family cat, but no one ever listens to me."

"Why would we if you spout such bile?" Eve's eyes spat like camels. "Ahh, here comes Bertie!" Livia was apparently distracted from the brief argument by the arrival of a well-dressed, ruddy-cheeked chap who was approximately forty per cent smile.

"Hello, my dear gentlemen." Every word he said came out as a chuckle. "What an absolute pleasure to have you here. The great Lord Edgington and…" Not knowing my name, he replaced it with an extra laugh.

"This is my grandson and assistant, Christopher." My grandfather often sounded inexplicably proud when he spoke of me. The only remarkable thing I had achieved in life was to be born into the Cranley family, and yet he seemed to think I possessed hidden talents. I had to hope he was right as, no matter how hard I looked, I was yet to find any. "And you are?"

"The name's Bertie." He came closer to shake my hand. In fact, his grip was so tight and his movement so impassioned that he shook my whole body, too. "Bertie Peregrine. Though my friends call me Bertie."

He was quite possibly the strangest of the lot, though I couldn't deny there was something charming about him. He rather reminded me of the Ghost of Christmas Present from Dickens's 'A Christmas Carol'. He was larger than life and had quite the same "unconstrained demeanour" as that happy spirit. He instantly turned the dinner into a party, and I was happy to have him there.

"Bertie is my husband." Eve stated this fact in a tentative manner, as though unsure of how she felt about the matter.

"And I can't begin to imagine what I did to deserve such a creature. I have worshipped her some forty years now, and I won't give her up without a fight." He beat me about the back and, though it left me a little numb, I found myself laughing along with him.

"Are you a writer too, Mr Bertie?" I don't know how I managed to mangle his name. He'd stated it quite clearly.

"Not at all, Mr Christopher." From now on, you can assume that every word he spoke was punctuated, and in some cases punctured, by raucous bursts of laughter. I had never met such a contrasting couple. "I'm a land agent. I sell fields and houses – that sort of thing."

"I have some questions for you, Lord Edgington." Livia fetched a pad and pencil as an impeccably dressed maid served an amuse bouche of sardine and tomato paste on walnut bread. It was much better than it sounded, and I began to enjoy myself. I was almost tempted to have a glass of wine but remembered just in time that I couldn't stand the stuff.

"Perhaps we should explain," the most authoritative sister, Nessa began. "We invite a different guest to dinner once a month and Livia here has been desperate to have you. I hope you don't mind her directness."

It was clear that Livia's sisters were used to speaking about her as though she wasn't there. For her part, the mystery novelist stared into space as though she hadn't heard. It was hard for me to imagine such a simple-minded woman being a great spinner of yarns or conceiver of puzzles, and it made me want to read her books even more.

"I am happy to entertain you in any way you wish," Grandfather replied, before looking about the room as if noticing his surroundings for the first time.

On the extensive tour, I had heard so much about the history of each ornament and dish in the room that I had failed to take in what a pretty space it was. The walls were covered in wooden panels which reached to the ceiling and were crowned with carvings which depicted scenes from an ancient Greek feast. They reminded me of how hungry I had become, and I was relieved when the next course was served.

"My first question," Livia said, and I noticed a glimmer of wisdom hiding within her after all. "Could you tell us about your most perplexing case of murder?"

"No, no, no!" Eve interrupted. "First, you must tell me who on earth you are. Or rather, I've heard your name often enough from my middle sister, but I'm not one for crimes and criminals. You had better introduce yourself, or I'm likely to fall asleep by the time the fish course is served."

"Now, my darling," Bertie admonished her. "There's a polite way to express such thoughts. I'm sure you didn't mean to sound rude, but—"

"Of course I didn't." The hatchet-faced woman even snapped at her own husband. "If Lord Edgington really is a living, breathing legend as Livia claims, he is an intelligent chap, and won't be offended if I forego the odd nicety."

Bertie and Nessa could only shrug and await my grandfather's reaction, and I must say that I was eager to witness it for myself. As bizarre as our company was that night, those people had nothing on my own mercurial companion.

He sat back in his seat, raised his chin to regard his inquisitor through the narrowest slits of eyes and adopted a persona I had never known before. "Very well, if you prefer honesty to good manners, I don't mind telling you that I am the greatest detective of this century." His words were dripping with arrogance, even by his immodest standards. "Not only did I spend forty years as an officer of the Metropolitan Police, in that time, I worked my way up from the lowest rung of the ladder to become a superintendent. Furthermore, during my retirement, I have brought to justice some of the most devious murderers in Britain, and I have yet to encounter a case that could fox me for long."

Perhaps it was the intensity of his uniquely grey eyes as he spoke, but Eve could do little but shiver in reply. A dry click emerged from her throat, and I thought she might attempt an answer, but no further comment came.

"Is that what you had in mind, or were you hoping for something else?"

CHAPTER FOUR

After this tense exchange, I was relieved that the conversation settled into a steadier rhythm. What's more, Livia began to show that there was more going on in her head than her family would allow. She had any number of well-composed points to put to the famous detective, and I think that even her overly serious sisters were a little impressed.

It was Grandfather himself, though, who illuminated that pleasantly old-fashioned room.

"Before we go any further, I should tell you about one particularly interesting case I came across in the slums of East London in the 1890s. There was a pair of twins known as the Nichol Brothers. Ross and Mick were identical, and the only way you could tell them apart was the patch over Mick's eye, which he was said to have lost in a knife fight.

"With their cut-throat gang, the brothers were the scourge of London. They robbed, cheated, swindled and stole. Not a building was safe from their schemes, be it a bakery in Cheapside or the vault of the Bank of England. So great was their fame, in fact, that most police officers were too scared to go into the Old Nichol slum, for fear of what might happen.

"There came a time, though, when we in the police could no longer ignore their crimes. You see, in the course of robbing a jeweller in Hatton Garden, one of the brothers shot a man dead. I led the squadron that was charged with bringing them to justice, and a witness had reported seeing Ross fleeing the scene of the murder. We went in with truncheons aloft and stormed their street."

He paused at this moment to ensure that every person at the table was enraptured by his tale. He needn't have worried. We'd each of us travelled back in time to that fateful day and were longing to hear the resolution.

"I planned the raid for early in the morning, in the hope of catching the brothers by surprise. We certainly roused the neighbourhood with our boots on the cobblestones, shouts of warning and the clatter of banging doors. But when we penetrated the gang's inner lair, only Mick was to be found. He swore he'd had nothing to do with the attack on the poor jeweller and, though we had no evidence to link him to the crime, we took him in for questioning. It was a shameful day for me, I can tell you. Ross had been spotted in the Old Nichol after the murder, but, though we turned the place upside down, and my informants swore that he couldn't have got away, our search was in vain.

"I went back to my office in Scotland Yard and sat at my desk, wishing that I'd been that little bit faster, imagining an explanation for the killer's escape, and trying to make sense of how we could have been so wrong."

There was a lull then, as we considered that this anecdote might end on a low note. I should have known my grandfather better than that. Just at the moment when it appeared that each member of his audience had given up hope of a neat conclusion, he asked us a question.

"And after two long days reflecting on my failure, do you know what I realised?" He looked around the five faces that reflected his curious expression back to him.

I could tell that this was not just a rhetorical question; he had set us a riddle and expected us to solve it just as he had.

"Was the chap stashed away in some sort of underground cell?" Nessa suggested. "Hidden beneath a thick carpet, perhaps?"

Grandfather shook his head and waited for another guess.

"Had he never returned in the first place, or slipped away in the dark?" There was a vein of arrogance in Eve's voice which suggested she knew better than the rest of us, even as she gave the wrong answer.

"No. We ruled out both possibilities. And, though I would otherwise have feared that the Nichol Brothers had paid one of my men to feed them information, I had set my best officers to keep guard over the streets around the slum and I trusted them implicitly."

"Some sort of tunnel, then?" It was my turn to have a stab at it. "You often read about tales of enterprising prisoners escaping from their cells. Could that be the explanation?"

Grandfather replied in a whisper. "No, but it's a good guess."

He had his eyes on Livia, who stared straight back at him. For a moment, I thought she might have struck upon a solution, but she shook her head in her usual absent-minded fashion, and it was clear that Grandfather would have to put us out of our misery.

He placed his fingers together above his plate of lamb casserole and I knew just how much he was enjoying his moment in the glare of our collective gaze. "The fact is that Ross had always been the more violent of the two brothers. Mick was in charge of running their operation, whereas Ross dealt with the other members of the gang and carried out the worst of their crimes. There was really very little with which we could charge Mick. To all intents and purposes, he was little more than an office boy, and we would have had to release him if I hadn't realised one important fact."

There was another pause as Grandfather's impressive moustaches bunched together in glee. "I ran down to the cells in Scotland Yard and demanded that the sergeant on duty open Mick's cell. I was brave but no fool and didn't go in alone. In fact, it took three officers to subdue the man as I removed the patch from his eye."

"They'd swapped places." I exclaimed after he'd given us all the relevant information we required to solve the crime. "Ross carried out the raid on the jewellers, did away with his brother, then put on a patch to make it look as though he was poor, innocent Mick." I was rather pleased that I'd managed to get this far.

"Oh, how clever," Eve, of all people, cried. "You would never expect that sort of person to have such brains in his head. Bravo."

There was a buzz and hum of appreciation, which Grandfather silenced with one raised hand.

"Not quite." He looked from face to face in expectation. "The two brothers didn't swap places, because there was only one of them from the start. Soon after his career as a criminal had begun, Mick Stevens had invented an alias for himself, and people had assumed that he was his own brother. No one ever saw them together, but with the simple disguise and the fear he could strike into his companions, no one dared question him. Mick had known there would come a time when he would need to escape his misdeeds, and so he made sure that Ross was the only one culpable.

"In his cell that day, I ripped the patch from his face and discovered a fully working eye. He was his own scapegoat. And with this knowledge, I managed to get the man sent to prison for life. He was only spared the gallows as the jeweller had been killed with his own gun, and we couldn't prove that the murder was intentional. London was certainly a safer place once the Nichol Brothers had disappeared from the streets – in Ross's case, quite literally."

Bertie was the first to react. He pounded his hands together, nearly spilling his wine in the process. "Bravo! Bravissimo, in fact. What a story and what a teller. I can't imagine that Captain Hardjack would have regaled us in such a way. I've rarely been so enthralled."

The two elder Shipley sisters echoed his applause, but Eve still looked unimpressed. "I suppose it's entertaining enough if you enjoy that sort of thing. I can't honestly say it thrilled me. Surely it was the job of the police to uncover such a ruse from the beginning. How did the chap get away with it for so long?"

"Do be quiet, Eve," Livia responded, her face still etched with delight. It was a triumphal moment, not just for my grandfather but for the mystery writer, too. I had to wonder whether she'd ever stood up to her overbearing sister before. Perhaps my grandfather's presence there had buoyed her spirits.

"I have a question for you next," Eve said, to turn the tide back the way it had come. "If you're such a mastermind at solving crimes, why don't you help plan one?"

Grandfather sat up straighter in his ornate wooden chair. As good humoured as he tended to be, he rarely made light of his profession. "I beg your pardon, madam?"

"I'm talking about the perfect crime." She enjoyed the impact that these words had on her audience. "It's one thing to solve a murder, but surely a truly great detective should be able to get away with one."

CHAPTER FIVE

Silence gripped the room, and I was uncertain how the matchless Lord Edgington would react to Eve Shipley's curious request. Even Bertie looked a little grim just then, and his eyes fell to the plate in front of him.

"The perfect crime," Grandfather repeated noncommittally. "It's an interesting concept, but I've yet to see any proof that such a thing exists."

"Oh, come along, man." Eve would not withdraw her challenge. "There must have been cases you couldn't solve. What marked out those from any other?"

He ruffled his long beard with the tips of his fingers and considered the question. "I'm afraid to tell you that it is not quite so fascinating as you might imagine. The majority of murder cases that go unsolved have one rather mundane factor in common. Almost invariably in such instances, it is due to the fact that we cannot rule out suicide as a cause of death and cannot launch a murder investigation as we might otherwise."

"There you go then. Simply make it look as though the victim has killed himself and you'll get off scot-free." Eve turned away as though the matter was now resolved, and we could move on to another topic.

Grandfather was quick to disabuse her. "Oh, no, no. That is far from true. In fact, when a murderer attempts to stage a suicide, he rarely succeeds. The killer will forget a minor though significant detail, such as whether the victim was right or left-handed. We must also remember that killings are often crimes of passion; it is exceedingly difficult to make a murder appear as a suicide after the fact."

"In what way?" Livia was all ears and had been scribbling in her notebook throughout the discussion.

The lordly visitor shifted in his seat before responding. "Well, if someone has been shot, you cannot simply place the gun in his hand, write a quick suicide note and hope that the police will accept the picture you have painted. The angle the bullet entered the body will most likely be unnatural, your handwriting will not match the victim's and in today's modern age of advanced scientific techniques, the chances are you'll have left any number of clues behind to connect you to the crime."

I could see that, of the three sisters, Nessa was the most patient listener, but she now spoke up. "So, what you're saying is that a good murder should be planned precisely?"

Grandfather clicked his fingers and pointed across the table with some glee. "Correct. If we are to land upon the perfect crime, we must ensure that two factors are brought into play. First, there must be the element of doubt; the possibility that it is not a murder at all, but a mere accident or misadventure."

"And second?" Eve enquired, her concentration now heightened, and her eyes fixed on the expert with some intensity.

"Second, there must be a more likely suspect ahead of you in the queue." With this answer provided, the atmosphere in the room seemed to change. It was as though the glass box within which we'd been trapped had shattered and the air had come rushing in for us to breathe. Bertie even went back to his jovial outbursts.

"So the best thing would be to push your victim off a cliff while the fellow's enemy is close at hand."

"Indeed." Grandfather's shoulders had relaxed just a fraction, and I could see that he was enjoying the conversation once more. "In fact, I would say that may well be the definition of a perfect crime. Without witnesses, it would be very difficult to determine whether someone fell or was pushed. But it needn't be so obvious a scenario. I once found a woman face down in a metal barrel. She was a street dweller – a woman of no fixed abode who had suffered terribly at the hands of her violent husband over the years. Sadly, mere weeks after leaving him, she keeled over in a barrel full of water in a quiet alley.

"It was days before anyone found her, by which time much of the physical evidence had deteriorated. All we could say was that no water had entered the lungs, though that might have been in keeping with a heart attack or severe stroke. Her brute of a husband was the obvious suspect, of course, but there was little to prove his involvement. The irony was that, with the coroner returning an open verdict and the case effectively closed, the odious man could live with his guilt no more and committed suicide." He slowly ran one finger along the length of his well-defined jawbone as he recalled the details. "Or at least, that's how it looked to the police. We'll never know for sure what really happened."

I doubt I was the only one who shuddered a little as he finished this account. The idea of a multitude of murderers walking about England without fear of prosecution was too much to comprehend. I'm sure I would have dwelt upon this news for far longer if a pretty young nurse hadn't escorted the final member of the Shipley family in to see us at this moment.

"Daddy, you're here." As Nessa stood up to receive the old chap, she spoke like a child who had been separated from her father for a term at boarding school.

For his part, Royston Shipley showed no great emotion at the reunion. He had come just in time for dessert – burnt pears in sherry, yum and indeed yum! His eyes were filled with the sweet treat that sat steaming on the table, but he was unable to consume it without the help of his attendant.

I must say that, though I often complain if I miss a meal, poor Royston looked like he hadn't eaten in months. His grey suit hung from his body as if it had once belonged to a much bigger man. There was something quite skeletal about him; it was not just the skinny wrists that poked from his sleeves, but his sunken eyes and hollow cheeks. He was a ghost of a man.

"Daddy's not been in the best of health recently," Nessa said in a strained voice, then leaned in to speak to my grandfather as though sharing a secret. "The truth is that we owe our success to him. Few fathers in the last century would have insisted that their daughters pursue a classical education or supported them in their literary endeavours. He taught us himself until we were ten and then made sure to employ the best teachers available."

My own aged gent turned to face the invalid. "It is a pleasure to be here, Mr Shipley. A genuine pleasure, and your accomplished daughters are a testament to the education with which you endowed them. Even today, many fathers fail to see the value that women offer to society." I think he would have kept chattering on in the same vein, but it was clear that Mr Shipley was too busy to react. He stared blankly as another spoon of dessert was manoeuvred into his mouth.

"What about travel?" Eve switched the theme of the discussion. She was a single-minded woman who thought nothing of the enjoyment of those around her and was only concerned with her own narrow range of interests. "Have your investigations taken you to any far-flung places? Mesopotamia, Baghdad, the Caribbean?"

Grandfather closed his eyes before answering. "I am a great traveller of the mind. Though I have never set foot on foreign shores, I have studied many countries in great detail from the comfort of my library and read about any number of fascinating sites and sights."

Eve struggled to comprehend his answer and pressed him once more. "What of Frankfurt then? You must at least have been to Germany."

"Really, Eve," Nessa complained. "You are a bore when the moment takes you. We could be here all night listing places that Lord Edgington hasn't visited."

Grandfather opened his eyes and displayed a sympathetic look. "I cannot say that I have even been to the continent. I know that my grandson here longs to travel, and I may yet take him on a grand tour of Europe, but there is so much to see here in Britain that it will take some persuading to get me to set sail."

My ears certainly pricked up at the idea of foreign travel. Until now, the former shut-in had just about embraced the idea of a short sojourn in Wales, so the idea of a voyage through such exotic lands as France, Spain and Belgium came as something of a surprise.

"But what about—" It was clear that Eve would not relinquish the topic and Nessa had to intervene once more.

"Really, that's enough!" The vicious tone she adopted was quite unexpected, and all heads swung in her direction. "We brought our guests here to learn about their lives, not persecute them for details that don't actually exist."

Her words rattled off the plates on the dresser (which, according to Eve's extremely thorough tour, had once belonged to Richard Brinsley Sheridan's granddaughter) and bounced from wall to wall like a tennis ball. They left behind an even frostier atmosphere than we'd previously experienced, and I tried to think of something that would break the tension.

Instead, Nessa and Eve glared at one another like a pair of hounds preparing to fight in some East End gambling den. Bertie released a nervous titter, which led to the only full sentences I would hear from the patriarch of the family that night.

"Why is he always laughing?" He looked around the table in search of an answer. "I don't see that he's got any reason to be cheerful. If I were him, I'd be downright—"

"Thank you, Daddy!" Nessa's temper clearly hadn't cooled, and she directed it down the table to her elderly father. Even the nurse who was attending him looked startled by the turn of events, and it fell to Livia to calm the storm that had risen.

"Perhaps we could ask Christopher here something about his ambitions in life. It is not often we spend time with a member of the younger generation, and I'm sure he'll have something interesting to tell us."

Everyone turned to look at me then, and I didn't have the first imaginings of what they might want me to discuss. Anything was better than that unbearable silence filling the room once more, though, and I gave it my best shot.

"I finished school a few months ago and really don't know what I want to do with my life, but I'm lucky enough to have a grandfather who believes I have potential. He thinks that I could become a good detective, even though I've never solved a case for myself and generally strike upon ideas that are quite far from the truth."

Perhaps it was my naivety, or my innocent tone, but the longer I spoke, the more my audience warmed to the discussion. Bertie let out a laugh that was far jollier than the last he'd managed, and even old Royston gave a short, "Pears, yum!"

Suddenly, the room was full of questions.

"How interesting." Livia picked up her pencil again. "And do you actually wish to become a detective, or is it merely your grandfather's idea?"

"What about an education?" Nessa added. "Have you not considered university? I believe that Cambridge offers a wonderful bachelor's degree in history if you were so inclined."

"Travel!" was all Eve could say at first, but she hurriedly followed the exclamation with a question of her own. "I concur with your plan for a voyage across Europe, and I must ask whether you have considered the Orient Express. That would be the perfect start to a journey should you wish to Asia. There's nothing like it, though I'd ideally like to visit South America next. Travel truly broadens the mind."

I really didn't know what to say to any of that, but Grandfather gave me an encouraging wink, and I answered them as best I could.

"They are all interesting points, and I've certainly considered them. In fact, I have no trouble finding good ideas for what I might like to do with my time. The problems only arise when I have to choose one."

This led to laughter from all sides of the long table (an eighteenth-century piece, which Eve insisted had been purchased from Lord Byron's cousin). Even the invalid had a chortle, and the conversation continued like that for some time.

But when the cheese course had been consumed and the adults' snifters of brandy were drained, silence fell. As we rose to retire for the night, I spied a few nervous glances, and I had the definite sense that our hosts were recalling the macabre discussion that Eve had initiated. I'm rarely right in my ideas, and even less often confident one way or another, but by the time I left the room, I felt quite certain that every last person there was wondering the same thing; who among us was capable of carrying out such a crime?

CHAPTER SIX

The house looked far more sinister by candlelight, and I was nervous that Martin the ghost would take a break from his usual stomping ground and swoop down to haunt us. My grandfather and I followed our amiable host Nessa up to the first floor and entered our rooms in the westernmost part of Pearson House. They were located in the Victorian wing that had (thankfully) been left off Eve's tour. They were decorated in much the same style as the rest of the property, with bare wooden beams in the low ceilings and far too many wardrobes, bureaus and cupboards crammed in to the space. It felt as though we were staying in a furniture shop.

I said goodnight to Grandfather and went off to cower in my bedroom, as the sounds of the house made me even more anxious. It was not just the creaking floorboards and squeaky hinges on every door that unnerved me. Whenever someone turned on a tap, the pipes in the whole property clanged as though an endless rush of demons was passing through them. And as for the toilets, let me just say that I've come across quieter fireworks in my life than the immense bang, crank, thud that greeted each pull of a chain.

I must have become accustomed to all the percussive noises as I did eventually fall asleep. I woke the next morning not to the sound of angry pipes or the tread of some unknown creeper, but a skin-curdling scream. Wait a moment, can skin curdle? Does that make any sense in the slightest?

Either way, it was a scream I heard coming from the floor above. A young woman's scream, to be precise, and it did not take a genius to realise that, considering the advanced age of the three sisters, it had come from one of the servants. I dashed out of my bedroom, but my grandfather was already ahead of me and reached the stairs to the top floor a few seconds before I could.

"Much as I suspected, Christopher," the old genius exclaimed, "We were brought here for a reason." He did not wait for my reaction but veritably thundered ahead.

The scream had died, but we found Royston Shipley's nurse quite distraught, collapsed on the bed where her patient should have been.

Though he had no formal medical training, Grandfather was blessed with a wonderful bedside manner. He checked her pulse and breathing before administering a cold flannel. I noticed that he also scanned a small row of brown glass bottles on the night table, perhaps in search of something to calm her nerves.

This gave me time to take the short, but apparently endless, walk to the latticed casement window that stood wide open. A crisp wind rushed over the low windowsill and into the small, featureless room. I couldn't help but shiver as I walked closer in nothing but my pyjamas, dressing gown and night cap.

When I reached the window, instead of peering at the ground below, it took me a few moments to drum up the courage I required. I scanned the horizon and the capacious garden that surrounded the property. At any other time, I would have greatly enjoyed carelessly exploring its acreage with our dog, but it was clear now that I missed my chance. I knew even before I looked at the old man, splayed out on the ground three floors below, that we had a murder to solve.

It was not until my grandfather finally joined me, his hand coming to a rest on my shoulder and his breath in my ear, that I fully accepted what had happened.

"The perfect crime," I whispered, and I wondered whether my learned mentor was thinking the same thing.

"The window is low enough that he could have fallen through it." He did not sound convinced, and we stood there reflecting on the possibility.

This moment of stillness was to be treasured as the house about to burst into life. I spotted Eve and Bertie down on the lawn, hacking over towards the crime scene. I could only conclude that the nurse's wail hadn't reached them as their hands were interlinked, and they wore matching smiles that would soon disappear. The youngest Shipley sister was the next to scream. The piercing noise Eve emitted echoed around the grounds, and she fell to her knees beside her lifeless father.

"Don't touch a thing," Grandfather exclaimed from on high, and I noticed that Bertie gripped his wife's shoulder to stop her from collapsing onto the body. "Christopher, watch them until I get downstairs. I will not have anyone interfering with the scene of the crime."

I hesitated before replying but found that I could not hold back the question for long. "So you do think he was pushed?"

Grandfather froze for a fraction of a second and gave a stern look that told me all I needed to know. He was dressed in his usual grey morning coat, which suggested that he had been awake and ready to face the world, while I was still blissfully exploring the land of Nod. Its long tails billowed around him as he spun through the door and out of sight.

I focused on the task he had assigned me and immediately heard the sound of another window opening. Livia Shipley was leaning out of her bedroom on the first floor. I assumed she was stunned by the sight of her dead relative, but it was not disbelief that shaped her features; it was a total absence of emotion. I wondered then if she felt so little for the man who had raised her, or she merely needed time to make sense of what she was seeing. In either case, the only woman there who was known to have plotted countless murders immediately shot to the top of my list of suspects.

Nessa was the last member of the family to see the body. She emerged from the house with my grandfather at her heels, as though still fulfilling her duties as our host. The calm, considered manner in which she strolled along the terrace suggested that she might just as well have been showing her guest where to sit for breakfast or pointing out a pretty walk he should take.

It was only when Delilah appeared from the front garden and began to bark at the dead man that reality struck. Nessa stopped right where she was, and her gaze fell upon her father. It was not my grandfather's job to comfort her. He was busy analysing every square inch of the scene in front of him. And yet, he was a kind man and, as no one else would do it, he reached out his hand to her. Nessa immediately put her head on his shoulder to cry. Even as she did so, Grandfather glanced towards the open window from where the owner of Pearson House must have fallen. He gave a perfunctory nod in my direction, and I knew that he required me at his side.

As I have already stated, this was not the first murder I had investigated with the eminent Lord Edgington, and a strange mix of emotions ran through me. As I sped down the various staircases of that extremely crooked house, I did not want to admit to myself that I was excited to delve into the mystery before us, and yet my nerves were firing like rifles at a… well… a firing range, I suppose.

Fear, apprehension and anticipation fermented within me, and I was eager to learn my grandfather's thoughts on what was, at the very least, a suspicious death. I was an amateur; a mere hobbyist when it came to solving crimes, but he was an expert by any definition of the word. I knew he would get to the bottom of whatever had occurred there in the time it took me to tie my shoelaces.

Livia was out in the garden when I arrived, and I'd spotted the Pearson House maid on the phone to the police. Grandfather had handed over his role as Nessa's proverbial (but also literal) shoulder to cry on to her younger sister. Bertie, meanwhile, without a single laugh, shepherded the three sisters along the patio and into a sitting room we had visited the night before.

I looked at the corpse and felt terribly blue about the world. Old Royston was face down on the paving slabs. His arms were loose at his sides and a faint trace of red had discoloured the stones around his head. But that wasn't the only thing that made me sad. What pained me so was the idea that the life of a good, accomplished man, who had done so much for his children, could end in such an ignominious fashion.

I considered for a moment who the likely suspect could be and was torn between Eve and Livia. But then, what do I know? Perhaps Grandfather had detected some hidden motive for Nessa Shipley's outburst at dinner. Or perhaps I knew nothing, and the young nurse was to blame.

"It's interesting, don't you think?" he enquired in a low voice once the others were out of earshot.

"Yes, of course I do. However, I feel that we're using that word far too often. Can't we at least think of a synonym?"

"You may have a point." He didn't move for three seconds and then started the conversation again. "It's intriguing, don't you think?"

"That's much better, thank you." I cleared my throat and answered his question. "And yes, it is a most intriguing case, indeed." A point of order occurred to me. "Would it not have taken some considerable force to move the victim from his bed and push him to his death?"

He took a few steps sideways to view the body from another angle. "I doubt that Royston Shipley weighed more than eighty pounds. I'm afraid we cannot rule out any of the members of the household so easily."

This opened a whole raft of possibilities, and so I looked for another way to reduce our list of suspects. "If I'm not mistaken, his death fits the parameters of the crime you outlined at dinner yesterday evening."

He breathed in through his nose, almost as though he wished to sniff out some elusive clue. "In that it will be difficult to determine between murder and the accidental death of a weak old man who fell through a low window? Absolutely. There is also a very real chance that the crime was not committed by the likely suspect. So, yes. The killer certainly adhered to the plan I described."

"If that was the case," I began a little hesitantly, as I was forever afraid that he would dismiss my suppositions as the work of an ill-informed child, "it would surely mean that Bertie or one of the three sisters are to blame for the death. They were the only ones in the room when you detailed your conception of a perfect crime."

"Yes, Christopher." His voice was bright, despite the sad scene on the ground in front of us. "Unless, of course, one of the domestic workers listened at the keyhole, it seems likely that we can restrict our investigation to the four members of the family with whom we dined." He moved his lips from side to side as though attempting to make his moustache perform a shimmying dance. "Which means we have already eliminated one third of our suspects. At this rate, we'll be finished in time for lunch."

"I haven't even had breakfast yet!" I might have sounded a touch pernickety, but he was forever making me skip meals and I did not like it one bit. "To be honest, I think it's terribly selfish that so many people insist on being killed at night. Why doesn't anyone consider my waistline? They say that breakfast is the most important meal of the day. I'll waste away if I have to miss any more of them."

Kneeling before the body, he extricated the soft white gloves from his pocket. "You've raised a significant point, Christopher."

I was terribly heartened by this. "So should I get the maid to tell the kitchen to start cooking?"

He sighed a long, troubled sigh. "No, boy, I mean that we must determine when exactly Royston Shipley fell to his death. It might enable us to rule out a suspect or two." He pulled back the high collar of the dead man's pyjama blouse in order to better see the condition of the corpse. "There is no sign of rigor mortis, for one thing, and little discolouration to the skin itself. I would say that he hasn't been dead for more than an hour, but there's something rather fascinating about the body. Look at the position in which he landed. What does it tell you?"

He was awfully good at putting me on the spot with such questions. More often than not, I would blurt out the first ridiculous idea that came into my head. In this case, the first thought I had was, *he appears to have fallen some way from the window. Perhaps he took a running jump.* With such nonsense safely dismissed, I could move on to more sensible solutions.

"His arms," I finally remarked. "They're at his side."

"Indeed. And what does that suggest?"

I walked around the body. "Yes… I think… Well, it seems to me that anyone falling from such a height would instinctively have held his hands out to protect himself. It wouldn't have done much good, of course, but it's human nature all the same."

"And so that tells us…"

"It tells us that he was not conscious when he took the plunge."

Grandfather rose and stuck his hand out over the corpse. I don't believe we'd ever shaken hands before. I can't tell you how proud it made me feel.

"A most astute observation, Christopher. Furthermore, we can see that the poor man has fallen some way from the house. If we rule out the possibility that he went for a running jump through the window, it would seem to confirm the hypothesis that he was pushed."

"Oh, you are droll." I emitted a truly sheepish laugh and was thankful that none of the deceased's loved ones were present to hear me. "Imagine even considering a man in his condition running about the place. The very idea is laughable."

As Grandfather spoke, his eyes were forever alert and traced the lines of the scene, much as an artist might sketch out a composition before painting. "But let me ask you this, can we say with absolute certainty that we are investigating a murder? Might it yet be an accident?"

Again, I got through my first idiotic thought and moved on to a second, more appropriate response. "If the window was open, Royston could have been sleepwalking and fallen to his death."

"Perhaps. And I have no doubt that, if we ask his nurse whether her patient was a somnambulist, she will reply in the affirmative."

I took a few brief moments to consider this. "How can you be so sure?"

"It's simple. Either he fell from the window in his sleep – perhaps tripping over the low windowsill which might feasibly explain the distance he landed from the house – or the killer was relying on this information to explain his relatively untimely death."

"Oh, how clever, Grandfather. You really do think of everything."

He stepped around the body and took my arm for support. Though he walked with his usual amethyst-topped silver cane, I was convinced it was merely a prop to set our suspects off guard. He was fitter than I was!

"No one can think of everything, my boy. But we can try our best to consider the many variables in the case. In fact, as I didn't have time to teach you to use my pistol, let this be your first lesson: we must forever imagine the unimaginable and consider the improbable."

I rather wished I'd had something with which to note that down. Instead, I stored it away in my brain for future reference. "Wonderful. So what's next?"

He had been walking towards the French doors of the sitting room but came to a stop. "I would think that was obvious. All we really know of our victim is his name, address and next of kin. It's time we filled in the rest of the details. It's time we spoke to our suspects."

CHAPTER SEVEN

It was also time for Grandfather to make use of his theatrical instincts. I had often pondered exactly why he hadn't pursued a career on the London stage. I had come across few actors with such poise, presence and precision of performance. He was a born thespian and, the moment we stepped inside Pearson House, his light, affable air disappeared, and a grave expression took possession of his features.

"A perfect crime," he declared in a gravely rasp. "That was the expression you used, was it not, Eve?"

The family was spaced out on a three-piece suite around the large marble fireplace. Sitting with her husband, the youngest sister quaked in fear as the detective laid down this opening gambit.

"She was talking hypothetically, as I'm sure you're aware." Bertie squeezed Eve a little tighter as he came to her defence. "And besides, if she had any intention of murdering her father, why would she have broached the subject with you present?"

"That is an... *intriguing* point. Indeed, I have often wondered why any killer feels safe in a hundred-mile radius of the great Lord Edgington of Cranley Hall." My grandfather wasn't actually as arrogant as he sounded that weekend. In fact, I believe he was playing up to the sisters' expectations and going along with the melodramatic atmosphere he had already established. Why he decided upon such an approach, however, is quite beyond me.

"The only conclusion I have come to is that, like most people, killers are arrogant and believe that they will be the ones to show up my inferior skills of deduction once and for all." He allowed himself a smug grin – again, this was all part of his act... I think. "Sadly for them, I have yet to meet my equal."

Presumably feeling he had riled Eve enough, he moved on to the middle sister. "And what of you, Livia? If anyone were equipped to plot a murder, it must surely be a mystery novelist."

"Wait just one moment." Nessa stood up from the armchair where she'd been carefully listening to all that was said. I thought I caught a hint of the anger she'd displayed the previous evening, but she smoothed her chintz frock before continuing in her usual civil tone.

"Who can say that Father didn't merely fall from the window? He was unsteady on his feet and had been known to sleepwalk."

Grandfather turned to me before replying and offered a wink that was not visible to our suspects. I did not need an interpreter to understand this gesture. He was saying, *Didn't I tell you, Christopher?*

He looked back at his questioner. "If the topic of our conversation at dinner was not enough to raise suspicion, the fact that your father made no attempt to break his fall and landed sufficiently far from the house to suggest some force was used upon him might do it."

"But you can't be sure." Nessa remained on her feet, and I thought it interesting that she had not allowed Livia to speak. It mirrored Bertie's behaviour towards his wife, and I had to wonder whether the two members of the household with the largest personalities were attempting to defend their more introverted companions. "You can cast all the aspersions you like, but you simply cannot prove that Daddy was murdered."

"That's hardly surprising," I found myself declaring. "Surely that was the whole point of our discussion last night. But whoever is responsible won't get away with murder. My grandfather will work out which of you is guilty before the police even drive through your gate."

I sounded most confident on the matter, but then we heard the beep of a horn in the front garden, and we would soon discover that a detective from Ipswich happened to have a holiday home in nearby Southwold and had made it there in record time.

"I appreciate the faith you have in me, boy." Grandfather couldn't help smiling as he acknowledged my error. "But I think that such rapid work would be difficult even for me." He swished across the room towards the exit, and I stayed behind to keep an eye on our suspects.

I felt confident that, if I continued to make absurd statements like the one I had just uttered, they would greatly underestimate me. It was the perfect opportunity to catch them unawares. That being said, none of them did anything particularly incriminating and, in time, the maid brought in a tea tray with a plate of sugary butter biscuits upon it. With no thought for the manners I would normally possess in such an instance, I positively launched myself across the room to secure a few for myself. I'm sorry if that offends anyone, but some things are more important than etiquette, and almost all of those things are edible.

With these provisions devoured, I went back to watching each member of the family in turn. Livia still hadn't spoken but sipped her tea rather noisily, which led to the occasional tut from Eve. Bertie looked as though he felt he should engage us in conversation but, whenever he opened his mouth, he would change his mind and close it again. Nessa was easily the most distraught of the lot and would look up at the door whenever she caught a noise in the house, as though hopeful it was her father, back from the grave and better than ever. That didn't happen, of course. Not even Martin the ghost dropped by to share his commiserations.

For my own part, I wondered whether Grandfather wanted me to begin the interrogations. I couldn't land upon the right opening question, though, and was most relieved when he returned to address us.

"I think it would be best if you were to wait in separate rooms so that I can interview you one by one."

"Come along, man," Bertie said with a note of disbelief in his otherwise booming voice. "Do you really think that is necessary?"

"I'm afraid I do. I am not here to engage in a little light confabulation. Detective Inspector Tabert has put me in charge of conducting the interviews whilst he gathers information from the crime scene."

This led to a dissatisfied stir of chatter among the three chairs, and I was surprised to hear Livia raise her voice to be heard over it. "That's not standard procedure. Why would the police trust you?"

Grandfather tapped his cane a few times on the floor and replied with characteristic good cheer. "Oh, you needn't worry about that. It just so happens that D.I. Tabert's father was a young recruit in the Metropolitan Police as I was starting my career. I spotted the resemblance as soon as we met. Apparently, old Tabert the Tank, as he was known then, always spoke highly of me to his son.

"And besides, if we don't get anywhere this morning, the young detective will take over the case this afternoon. Now, if you could do as requested and move into one of the neighbouring rooms, I would be most grateful."

CHAPTER EIGHT

I was curious to know whom Grandfather would choose as his first interviewee. Livia remained the likely killer in my book, as she had bumped off so many poor souls in her own books. Eve had a wicked tongue and was far from a diplomatic presence in the family. But more importantly, as her husband had reminded us, she was the one who had first raised the concept of a perfect murder at dinner. We couldn't rule out Bertie either. No matter how cheerful a chap he was, there might still have been a cold-blooded assassin lurking within him.

The only thing I felt with any certainty was that Nessa Shipley, the much-admired historian whose invitation had lured us to the house the day before, was the least likely to be responsible for her father's death. For one thing, I'd seen the affection that she'd had for the sickly old fellow. And, though she was the eldest daughter, and therefore most likely to inherit the estate, she already lived there quite comfortably. So what good would killing her father do?

Thankfully, I wasn't alone in the investigation. Though it would have taken me all day just to choose our first witness, my grandfather knew precisely where to begin.

"I am terribly grateful for your seeing us like this, madam." He said with a truly majestic bow after we'd followed Nessa into the library. "I can only imagine how difficult this morning must be for you."

I'm rather partial to books, and they had a fine selection on display. Most libraries in the grand estates I'd visited tended to forego much in the way of literature in exchange for dusty tomes on science, politics, history and the like, but in Pearson House the classics were all represented, along with a truly comprehensive selection of crime and detective novels. I was torn between pulling down a first edition of Dickens's 'Little Dorrit' and a selection of works by that American chap, Edgar Allan Poe. My grandfather was something of an admirer of his, and I noticed a truly beautiful edition of the author's 'Tales', complete with gilt bordering and shiny beetles on the spine.

With no reply from our suspect, who had taken her place behind a grand Chippendale desk, Grandfather soon continued. "I feel that I must learn more about your father before we can successfully determine whether he was murdered. You mentioned that he was instrumental in your and your sisters' schooling?"

Nessa hesitated for all of three seconds before providing a full and authoritative answer. "That's correct. He felt that all children deserved the right to an education and treated my sisters quite the same as if we'd been boys. My mother agreed with him, of course, but she was a sickly creature and Eve's birth was too much for her. In fact, my father is the only parent I truly remember."

"You would say he was a good man, then?" She nodded in reply and so he rephrased the question. "Can you think of any enemies he might have had?"

Nessa turned to me at this moment. This was a common reaction from our suspects, but there was nothing I could do to help her. "Enemies? He'd barely left the house for a decade. I would struggle to name any of his friends, let alone an enemy."

"Jolly good." Grandfather had not sat down but brushed his gloved hands against one another, satisfied that he could move on to another topic. "I'm afraid that my next question pertains to the will. Can you tell me whether, as the eldest child, you will inherit the bulk of the estate? Or had your father made other provisions?"

Her eyes immediately hopped across the room to a wooden cabinet with countless drawers for storing documents. I could only assume that this was where we would find the last will and testament of Royston Shipley, though Nessa herself would furnish us with the information we required.

"His legacy is further proof that my father was no traditionalist. His estate and fortune will be split between his remaining children. We will all get the same amount of money now that he is dead. Should any one of us wish to dissolve the estate, we will be obliged to do so."

"How fascinating." Lord Edgington settled into a brown leather chair, which swivelled a few degrees as he landed on it.

Nessa was apparently encouraged by his response. "I cannot impress upon you enough just how forward thinking my father was. Royston Shipley was a man of grand ideas. Though born in the eighteen forties, he always looked to the future and taught his children to do the same."

My own father was almost fifty years younger than the dead man, and yet he still believed in the Victorian values with which he'd been raised. I found it rather wonderful to learn about such an enlightened gentleman as Mr Shipley. If anything, it made me sad that all I'd heard from him in life were a few mumbled expressions. I'd dismissed the old fellow as a spent force when he might well have been blessed with a brilliant mind to the day he died.

"And what of your relationship with him? What did he think of your success as an author, for example?"

Nessa was a truly expressive woman and appeared unable to resist any number of telling gestures. She pulled her shoulders back and looked at the bookshelf beside her. There was a small collection which bore her name, including books on royal families from England, Scotland and across the continent to Holland and Germany. A text on the English Civil War stood out to me but, more interestingly, the shelves beneath were filled with her sister's bibliography.

My eyes hungrily scanned the titles of Livia Shipley's books and I soon found 'The Seven Sisters of Solomon Leroux' that our chauffeur Todd had mentioned. Since I'd devoted part of my free time to chasing after criminals with my grandfather, I'd become something of a connoisseur of detective stories. While I very much doubted that Miss Shipley's novels could live up to the incredible new book from a certain Mrs Christie, I was eager to discover what literary traps she had fashioned for her readers.

"I loved my father, and he loved me." Nessa's voice struck through the conversation like a bolt of lightning on a clear day. I instantly forgot about fiction and concentrated on the drama unfolding before us. "Without him, I would never have become an author or even set pen to paper. While most girls from my youth were married off to the highest bidder, my sisters and I were given the chance to become significant figures in our chosen fields."

"You never married?" I thought this a rather churlish response on my grandfather's part, but then I can only imagine that was his intention.

"I never wanted to marry." Her face had turned from stormy to hurricane…y. "It may shock you to realise that not every woman requires a man to make her feel as though she has accomplished something."

He did not bite back immediately but licked his thumb to smooth one steel-wire eyebrow. "Do you think that is true of your younger sister? Do you believe that Eve married for such a reason?"

"I didn't say that." The more questions she answered, the more frustrated poor Nessa became. I saw her glance at a pile of ancient documents on the desk in front of her, and I knew that she would have preferred to be communing with long-dead figures from history than battling the bothersome detective. "In fact, if a good man like Bertie had come a-courting, I might very well have changed my mind. But that does not mean I lack for a husband."

The superlative Lord Edgington looked quite pleased with himself – just for a change. He had waved a red flag, and the bull had huffed and puffed but never charged. I knew just how exasperating the old fellow could be, and I was rather impressed that Nessa Shipley had shown such self-control. I could only think that, had she been guilty of the killing, Grandfather would have got the truth from her. Instead, she took a deep breath and asked a question of her own.

"Is there anything else you wish to know about my family?"

"Yes. How exactly did your father make his money? I know no Shipleys in the English aristocracy. He held no title, so I can only think he was some sort of…" He struggled over the next word and wore a disgusted frown as he pronounced it. "…*merchant.*"

It was another part of his act. I'd met snobbier postmen than the Marquess of Edgington, but Nessa was unaware of this and responded accordingly.

"You're absolutely correct in your inference and absolutely despicable in your tone. My father was the son of a wool merchant. He built up our family's fortune on the back of his own hard work and bought this house with the money he saved. It almost bankrupted him, but he wanted the very best surroundings for his children, which is exactly what he gave us. He wasn't just handed a fortune like some people."

It was interesting… no, wait. It was intriguing to see how quickly the polite mask Nessa had worn since our arrival had slipped. I had to wonder whether there was more to discover, simmering away beneath the surface. Some dark secret that would reveal hidden feelings for the dead man on the patio, the man she claimed to adore.

"Well, thank you. I have no intention of causing you any more suffering than you have already endured, and I am grateful for your time." I knew from his suddenly considerate tone that Grandfather's interview was not yet complete. He had one more tactic to employ, one more worm with which to bait her. "It must be a comfort to know your father thought highly of you." He fell silent for the count of five before delivering the blow. "Considering that your sisters are so much more successful."

The treacherous man before her had overstepped the mark, and Nessa needed to catch her breath. I was expecting a *how dare you?* Or perhaps an *I beg your pardon?* But, instead, our suspect turned her head to one side and re-evaluated her interrogator.

"You know, Lord Edgington, you're just as clever as everyone says. Livia had been begging for months to invite you, and even Eve was keen to discover what you knew about the world, but I resisted. I had the terrible feeling that you were all show and sparkle with little in your head worth investigating. Evidently, I was wrong."

"You are simply too kind, madam."

She nodded serenely, and I wondered what she had gleaned from his rudeness that I had failed to see. "You are a truly masterful puppeteer. In place of marionettes, you have the suspects in your cases. In place of strings, you pull at our emotions until we dance to the tune you have chosen. I'm really very impressed."

He released a silent laugh and crossed one leg over the other. "Impressed enough to answer my question?"

"Very well." She took in a slow breath through her nostrils. "I will answer the question which you devised for the sole purpose of unearthing any rivalries that may exist between my two sisters and me. I have no reason to be jealous of Livia and Eve, as it is my name that most people in this country know.

"My books have become synonymous with conscientious historical research backed up with solid evidence. Livia may have sold more books than me, but she does not possess the standing I have achieved. As for Eve, I will admit that she has a talent for setting tongues wagging with her lurid portrayals of foreign climes, but the public has already tired of such frivolities. As you will already know if you read The Times, the vilification of the Spanish people to which she stooped in her last publication was not well received."

She delivered her final defence with great poise and composure. "I have no reason to envy the backlash Eve received in the press, nor her subsequent poor sales. If anything, I pity her."

CHAPTER NINE

"Really, Grandfather, I think you are at risk of taking your harlequination too far."

I suspected that he would have some clever retort to fire back at me but, instead, he placed one hand on my shoulder, looked me deep in the eye and said, "I have no doubt that you're correct in your assertion, Christopher. But *harlequination* is not a word. Now, what did you make of the results of my most effective interviewing technique?"

"I think you took it too far." I removed his hand from my shoulder and his arm swung between us. We had retreated to the gardens to discuss the finer details of the case – and my grandfather's performance as a rude, provocative pest.

"While I concede that I may have given our suspect the impression that I was little but a deranged man barking at the moon, as I've told you many times, you can't make honey without bothering a few bees."

"I don't believe you've ever said that before."

He was pacing in front of the French windows we had just walked through but stopped to consider my response. "Haven't I? Well, I've certainly thought it a lot in your presence. The point is that difficult cases sometimes call for a difficult sort of detective. I may have to step on some toes and break some eggs in order to upset the apple cart and get to the truth. The fact that I have already annoyed my most faithful companion suggests that we are on the right path."

His pacing resumed. He only engaged in such activity when something was perplexing him, and so I was fairly confident that he was no closer to solving the case than he had been before Nessa's interview.

"Excuse me, Lord Edgington," a middle-aged chap in a thick woollen suit and a threadbare scarf called over. He'd been lurking beside the body with an equally poorly dressed companion, and I could only conclude this was Detective Inspector Tabert, whom Grandfather had previously mentioned. "The coroner is here. He's given me his notion of the time of death, and I thought you might like to know."

As he did not reveal the proffered fact, Grandfather encouraged him. "I certainly would."

"Very good, sir. Well, our man thinks that Mr Shipley fell from the window at close to seven o'clock this morning."

"I see." The more experienced of the two detectives considered this new piece of evidence as he drew a circle with his foot on the gravel path. "That's much as I suspected but still very interes— It's intriguing, nonetheless."

"That it is, sir. As is the statement I obtained from the dead man's nurse. She says that he was prone to sleepwalking, but she did not hear him leave his bedroom last night, and she is normally a light sleeper. She was in the room next door, but all she noticed this morning was the clanking of the pipes at five minutes past seven. She thought nothing of it and fell back asleep until eight when she went in to check on her patient."

"Then I feel yet more confident in saying that this is no accident we are investigating. Royston Shipley was murdered." I struggled to see what evidence the nurse's account had provided to promote this belief, but the conversation continued before I could analyse it any further.

"I was thinking the same thing, sir." Tabert had a rather flat face that looked as though it were in a state of permanent surprise. "The temperature fell sharply yesterday evening, and the nurse insists that she did not leave the windows open when she put the old man to bed. Still, we'll look into the other members of staff in case anything significant turns up in their pasts."

"That's fine work, Tabert. I appreciate the effort you've made." Grandfather almost literally sang the man's praises. I wasn't the slightest bit jealous. "Keep me informed of any further developments."

The two men nodded to one another, and Tabert seemed thrilled to have elicited such a response from the legendary officer.

"I don't understand why we started with Nessa Shipley," I decided to contribute once the shabby policeman had left. "We've found nothing to suggest she would wish her father any harm, and she's been the picture of a perfect host ever since we arrived."

Grandfather continued with his artistic endeavour, and the circle beneath his foot became a clockface. The small hand was pointing to the seven and the big hand to the one.

"You noticed nothing strange about her behaviour at dinner last night?" He spoke in a tone of pure bewilderment.

"I noticed that she showed a little anger at one moment, if that's what you mean. I would not say she betrayed a murderous nature, though."

"It was not her anger to which you should have been alerted, Christopher. It was to whom she directed her words. There is clearly a great rivalry between Nessa and Eve. And don't forget what I told everyone about the realisation of a perfect crime. It is not enough to make a murder look like an accident. There must also be a more likely suspect on hand to take the blame should your subterfuge be discovered."

He paused just briefly to allow me to consider the point. "Eve is a cantankerous, suspicious and largely unpleasant woman who brought up the topic of plotting a murder in front of everyone last night. She is a far more obvious culprit than our sweet friend Nessa, or their apparently less intelligent sister."

"But that doesn't explain what possible reason Nessa would have for killing her father."

Grandfather's forehead creased together like a concertina. "Doesn't it?" He gave me a few moments to feel stupid before revealing what he meant. "So you don't think Nessa would be happier inheriting half of her father's estate, as opposed to a mere third?"

I was about to say, *I don't understand,* but I knew my grandfather wouldn't like that and so I did some thinking out loud to make sense of his riddle. "You mean that, by murdering Royston and making her sister look like the guilty party, the blame would fall on Eve?"

"Precisely! And, as we both know, English law prevents an inheritance from being distributed to any person who can be shown to have brought about the death in question." I did not know this, but I wasn't about to tell him that. "Of course, we have only spoken to one of the people involved in the case. It could well be that a new likely option comes forward, or that Eve, knowing that we would suspect her, deflected suspicion onto Nessa based on the formula I had detailed."

This really needed some careful computation before I could respond. "So what you're essentially saying is that the killer could still be any one of them?"

He put his finger and thumb up to his chin and pinched together the ends of his beard. "Yes, that's exactly it. It could be any one of them."

I had a more concrete idea of my own to put forward. "What I don't understand is why you are so quick to dismiss Livia as our culprit. Surely her occupation makes her uniquely suited to plotting a murder. Didn't you notice that she noted down everything you uttered at dinner last night?"

I believe he was about to pooh-pooh my idea when Todd arrived with Delilah at his heel. Our chauffeur looked a little flustered, whereas our dog looked as though she wanted to chase a stick.

"M'Lord, I'm sorry if this is a bad moment, but I think I've discovered something rather important." He was gripping a slim grey book with the shape of a dagger inlaid on the cover in shimmering silver. "I heard from the kitchen staff about the master falling from the top floor of the house and… well, it reminded me of something."

He tentatively held out the book to us and I read the four words on the front. 'Eleven Ways to Die' was a morbid title if ever there was one, and I felt a buzz of excitement as I took the volume in my hand.

"I haven't the time to read a whole novel just now, Todd," my grandfather replied. "Perhaps you could give us a precis of the relevant parts."

"Of course, M'Lord. You see, the book takes place in a house much like this one. It's about a family of ten siblings and the middle sister kills the others off one by one."

I think I might have gulped just then. They did not appear to have heard, so I did it once again, a little more loudly. "You mean to say that Livia wrote a story that hints at what happened here before it occurred?"

Todd's face had turned pale. "More than that, I'm afraid. The father in the book dies in quite the same fashion as Mr Shipley did. He's pushed from a window and cracks his skull open on the ground beneath."

This would have been the perfect moment for the three of us to stand staring at one another in abject horror before rushing off to rake Livia Shipley over the coals. Rather disappointingly, there was an unfortunate interruption.

"I'm terribly sorry to bother you, chaps," Bertie Peregrine declared with a gigantic laugh that echoed about the garden. "It's just that, well, we've been waiting for some time to talk to you, and there's only so much a couple who've been married for forty years can talk about before conversation runs dry. If you're not too busy, I was rather wondering if you wouldn't mind seeing us next?"

CHAPTER TEN

The interview didn't start exactly as I'd imagined. In fact, Eve sat at the harpsichord and burst into song before Grandfather could ask his first question.

> **"Oh Mr Porter what shall I do?**
> **I want to go to Birmingham,**
> **And they're taking me on to Crewe.**
> **Send me back to London as quickly as you can.**
> **Oh Mr Porter what a silly girl I am!"**

"Thank you, madam. That was simply wonderful," he interrupted after the first chorus. "Now, if you wouldn't mind me—"

She rose to cut short his request. "Did you know that this harpsichord is over two hundred years old and was once on display in the palace of King Louis XV's neighbour?"

There was a moment's silence before my grandfather reluctantly replied with the truth. "Yes, I did. You told us last night."

"Well, really." Eve sounded more than a touch vexed. "You could at least pretend to be interested!"

She was clearly attempting to delay the interview we had come to the music room to conduct. Perhaps tired of hearing such tedious details, Bertie went to settle her down on a sofa and revealed what she could not say for herself.

"I have rather important news. We didn't mention it earlier, as we didn't know the time at which poor Royston died. But at seven o'clock this morning, we'd already left for our constitutional."

"Wait just a moment." I hated to wipe the carefree smile from his face, but... well, there was no other option. "How do you know that your father-in-law was murdered at seven—"

"Five minutes past seven, to be precise," my grandfather corrected me.

"How do you know when he died?"

Bertie looked a little sheepish. "That policeman chappy was talking to the coroner rather loudly outside our window. I'm afraid we couldn't help but overhear."

I clicked my fingers in disappointment. If anything, Grandfather seemed amused by this outcome. As though impressing upon me that he would now take his turn with our suspects, he squeezed my shoulder and took the floor.

The music room was well-named as it contained... well... a lot of instruments and the like. There were ancient lutes strung from the walls, a piano dominated one half of the room, and brass horns of every variety were stored on a low shelf for any musically minded visitor to use. I doubt that any of this was relevant to the case, though I thought it a pleasant space in which to carry out an interrogation.

"So you'd like us to believe you had already left on your morning walk at the time Royston was pushed to his death from a top-floor window?" I could tell that Grandfather had chosen these words to elicit a reaction and Eve quite jumped out of her skin.

"You don't have to believe it." She fixed her gaze upon her inquisitor as she stated her case. "It is the truth."

Standing against one wall, out of sight of the suspects, I watched Eve closely and thought I could perceive the slightest jerk in her muscles as she said this final word. Unlike my mentor, I was no expert on body language, but it made me question her story at least.

"To a detective, madam, truth is a relative concept. Even the most disinterested witnesses are likely to insert some faint bias into their testimony." He paused to let his meaning penetrate before returning to the details of the alibi. "Please tell me at what time exactly you left the house."

"It was half-past six at the latest," Bertie answered.

"That's right." I don't think Eve blinked the whole time we were in that room. "I would say it was half-past six by the time we were dressed and out of the door."

"Do you often get up so early to tramp about in the cold?" The idea was quite foreign to me.

Bertie was the first to respond, but his normally cheerful demeanour was muted, and he mustered little more than a thin smile. "My doctor says I should be doing more exercise, and my darling Eve kindly accompanies me. By getting up so early, we can be at home by the time Royston wakes—" He caught himself then and, with a swallowed breath, tried again. "By the time Royston usually woke up, we could be back at the house in case we were needed."

I risked another question of my own. "Eve, what was actually wrong with your father?"

She positively glared at me in response. "He'd been alive for almost a century. Everything was wrong with him."

I could see that, occasionally at least, Grandfather enjoyed my interruptions. He sat down beside the grieving woman to offer a word of comfort. "I'm sure that it must have been terrible to see a good man like your father grow old and infirm. Perhaps what happened this morning was a small mercy. So many men his age suffer long, drawn-out demises. I think I'd rather—"

"No!" she screamed, and this single word must have deafened the poor chap. "Daddy's death was no mercy, and I am not in any way responsible for what happened."

Grandfather tried another tack. "As I understand it, your father was a wealthy man, and you and your sisters are due to inherit equal shares of his fortune. I believe that much of his money was invested in this house, but I'm sure he's provided for each of you very well."

"What are you suggesting?" Bertie's voice rose in outrage on his wife's behalf.

Grandfather was a master of sly insinuation and, with one raised eyebrow, made his feelings quite clear. "I was merely wondering about your own financial situation."

Eve audibly huffed. "I'm dreadfully sorry, but I do not see what interest that is to a perfect stranger."

"A stranger who has been charged with investigating your father's murder? Oh, I think it has rather a lot to do with me." He dropped her gaze at this moment and paced the room as he detailed the first piece of evidence against her. "I have been informed that your last publication was a success neither critically nor commercially. I can only wonder at the impact that such a savaging in the press would have on your reputation, not to mention the sales of your books."

I saw Eve's indignation grow as she absorbed my grandfather's comments. "I can assure you that I have no fear for our economic security. My husband is a successful land agent. Tell them, Bertie."

She turned to her husband, who looked quite at sea. When he finally replied, it was in the most melancholic tone I had heard from him. "There's no sense in lying, darling. With a little investigation, the police will find out easily enough."

"Bertie!"

He turned to my grandfather before she could convince him to hold his tongue. "It is true, Lord Edgington. My business never recovered after the war. Our economic circumstances are not as good as they once were."

Eve could not hold her temper any longer. "None of this is relevant. The fact is that I did not murder my father, and your insensitive enquiries change nothing."

Grandfather dropped all attempts at delicacy and sought the answer we all wished to know. "So then, who is to blame?"

The question reared up between them, forcing Eve backwards against the sofa. It would soon grow and solidify, becoming a stone tablet, there for all to observe – a megalith in the middle of that well-appointed room.

"You can't expect us to do your job for you," Bertie replied.

It was clear, once again, that his instinct was to shield his wife from suspicion. I could only wonder where the line lay between protection and obstruction.

Grandfather was resolute. "That is not what I asked you to do. If, as you claim, neither of you were involved, I merely wish to know who you think could have murdered Royston Shipley?"

Eve's lower lip trembled. Her jaw fell a fraction and, in place of a reply, she emitted a haunted sound.

"I'm asking who you believe is capable of such savagery."

Inevitably, Bertie was the first to respond. "It must be one of the staff. No one in the family would hurt the dear old chap." His eyes darted about quickly at that moment. He was searching for something, and it occurred to me that, until now, he hadn't given much thought to who the killer might be. "His nurse perhaps? She seems like a nice young woman, but she only started working here in the spring. Isn't it possible she's done this sort of thing before?"

"No, it is not." The old detective's response was like a cricket bat to the gut. "The police will have looked into her credentials by now and, were anything unusual to be found, she would have been arrested. Besides, what would she gain from pushing an old man from a window?"

Eve clearly felt herself on steadier ground and stammered out a response. "You… well, you hear about people who take a perverse thrill from violence. That's the only explanation."

Grandfather turned away from them, the gesture a rebuttal in itself. "Oh, please. That is always the first response of the witnesses in any such investigation. People seem to believe that, all over Britain, madmen are running about murdering people for their own pleasure. And do you know why such ideas persist?"

He paused for a few ticks of a large clock on the wall behind him before answering the question. "They persist because it is far more comforting than the thought that someone close to them could be a killer. The nurse is no savage. Nor did your cook or maid take a brief jolly to the top floor this morning in order to murder their master. Royston was slain by a member of his own family. So if you're adamant that you are not responsible, tell me which of your sisters caused his death."

Silence greeted his furious entreaty. He would not move a muscle until one of them had spoken. His eyes budged not one eighth of an inch in their sockets.

I had assumed that Bertie would deliver another cheery though unhelpful comment, but it was Eve who found her voice. "I suppose it must be…" It didn't last long. Her words came to a sudden halt, and she stared up at the cloudy sky through the window.

"Say the name that came to your mind, Eve." Grandfather had softened his tone considerably. "Say what you were thinking. It does not mean that she will be arrested, but you must feel that one of your sisters is the more likely culprit."

As though her soul had been pulled back inside her body, she came to life and looked to her husband for reassurance.

"Say what you were thinking, darling," Bertie urged in a sad whisper. "Say the name."

"Livia." She let out a long breath, as though she'd been holding it in with her secret. "She has always possessed a morbid character. When we were children, she collected knives and old bullets and loved nothing more than to read the most violent penny dreadfuls. I'm afraid her obsession has only grown in later life. We should never have let her get carried away with all those sinister stories of hers."

Bertie seemed unsure how to react. On the one hand, he wished to support his wife, and yet his generous spirit meant that he could not bear to hear his sister-in-law's name besmirched. "I think if you'd read her books, you'd see that they have a real moral message to impart. They're not all blood and violence."

"Oh, please, Bertie." Eve unleashed a spike of anger. "She's a little savage, and you know it. As soon as I saw Daddy there on the paving stones, my mind went to Livia."

CHAPTER ELEVEN

"Grandfather?" I asked as we navigated the corridors of Pearson House. "Did you not recently tell me that we should not allow general impressions of a suspect's personality to influence our cases?" I took particular exception to Eve's use of her sister's slightly sinister childhood interests as evidence of her murderous nature. I had learnt from previous cases that such lazy thinking often led to incorrect conclusions.

"I may have said something along those lines." He chose his words carefully. "But it is not merely Eve's identification of Livia as the likely culprit that makes me suspect her. Don't forget the similarity between her father's death and the murder in the book that Todd had read. Livia would not be the first literary fantasist whose life came to mimic her books. Indeed, Oscar Wilde believed that 'Life imitates art far more than art imitates life.'"

"I don't think this is the time to ponder such highbrow notions." I possibly sounded a little petulant, but there was a killer on the property and… well, I considered that something of a problem. "Can we please concentrate on the case at hand?"

That was easier said than done as, before we could interview Livia Shipley, we had to find her. She was not in the sitting room where we'd last seen her, nor was she in any of the downstairs salons we had visited the day before. The dining room and kitchen were similarly eliminated from our search and, upon sending Nessa up to her sister's bedroom, we came to the conclusion that the mystery novelist was no longer in Pearson House.

Delilah dashed through the rooms we entered as though engaged in a particularly exciting game of hide and seek. She was quite overjoyed when it became clear that we would have to continue our hunt in the vast grounds of the estate. The rambunctious beast led the way across the substantial lawn, with its circular flowerbeds dotted here and there as though dropped in place by some gigantic passing bird. I doubt that she had picked up a scent as, despite being a fiercely loyal companion and a truly soft-hearted beast, Delilah was no great tracker. It finally fell to our master – well, her master and my mentor, but the relationship was really very similar – to point us in the right direction.

Even then, there were elm groves to traverse and winding paths to follow before we emerged beside the pond I'd noticed from the upstairs window. We found Livia sitting upon an old wooden bench, reading one of her own books.

"Good morrow to you both," she called in a cheerful voice. This led to a disgruntled bark from Delilah and our suspect soon corrected herself. "My apologies. Good morrow to the three of you."

Delilah was quite the most forgiving creature (and the best canine mathematician) I had ever come across. She immediately rushed over to Livia for a scratch behind the ears and some affectionate stroking. This brought to two the number of suspects I now felt compelled to exclude from our inquiry on the basis of their love of dogs. I just had to hope that Eve and Bertie were not similarly enamoured with Delilah, or we'd be back to where we'd begun.

"Good morning again, madam." Grandfather copied her airy tone and clearly did not intend to take her to task on her rebellious and unannounced flight from the house. To be perfectly honest, with several police officers on the premises, one might have hoped that an old lady would not have slipped away unnoticed.

"I suppose you're here to ask me whether I murdered my father." She did not sound intimidated by the possibility. If anything, there was an amused tone to her voice, as Grandfather sat down precariously on the stone rim of the pond.

"Well, did you?"

Livia demonstrated that incongruous slowness that we had witnessed in her the previous evening. It was hard to know whether it was part of an act, or it was down to a medical condition. It did not make sense to me that such a successful writer of complex novels could appear so... what's the word for it? Well, *stupid* is the obvious one, but that's a little rude. I have heard of idiot savants, of course, but isn't it also true that certain unlucky folk who have suffered head injuries can retain their facilities but struggle to express themselves? Perhaps that would explain her contradictory nature.

She raised her chin a little haughtily before finally responding to Grandfather's question. "No. I did not. I am not a violent person and wished my father no harm." There was a strangely hollow ring to her words, and I remembered the expression she had worn in her window that morning when she first spied the body.

"And yet, you didn't love him, either." I surprised my grandfather with these words, but he leaned back a little as though to give me the reins of the interview. I was rather worried he would fall into the pond!

"It is not an arrestable offence to feel no love for one's parents." What a cold fish she was. I'd found her rather sweet in a doddery, chaotic sort of way the night before, but I could not appreciate this unpleasant side to her.

"Would you mind explaining why you felt that way?" I continued. "It may not be a crime, but I'm sure you'll concede how unusual it is not to feel compassion towards your own father."

Again, she needed a quarter minute to formulate a response. Even Delilah found this strange. She kept looking between me and her new friend as if to say, *what's wrong with this woman?*

"I'll concede that most people claim to love their families. I, however, prefer to tell the truth."

"So the same holds true for your sisters?" Grandfather put in and, this time, she did not need to think about her answer.

She sighed a tired sigh, and I felt that we were seeing yet another facet of her shifting personality. "I'm sixty-eight years old. I've been living in this house all that time with my family around me. Presumably there are siblings who can still adore one another after so long, but I'm sure you can see that mine are rather... How should I put it? ...Peculiar, to say the least."

The inimitable Lord Edgington was apparently taken aback by her admission. I could only assume that his grand plan was, through a series of verbal tricks and traps, to prove that not everything in Pearson House was as harmonious as the sisters had simulated. Livia's unanticipated honesty had robbed him of his purpose.

"What...?" he began and then, raising one finger, he reconsidered the question. "Or rather, when...?"

"I think what my grandfather is trying to ask is whether you are aware that the death of your father is similar to the description of a murder in one of your novels."

"Similar? I'd say it was quite identical." She kept her eyes on my favourite old fellow, even as she answered me. "And, yes, thank you. I am familiar with my own body of work. Nessa even deigned to include copies of my novels in the family library."

"Don't you think it is something of a coincidence that life should mimic art quite so exactly?" I put to her, though I should have thought more carefully about how I phrased my question. I had no doubt that my grandfather had prepared a forthcoming lesson for me on that very topic.

"Yes, I do think it is something of a coincidence." Her voice retained its flat, rather lifeless quality, yet she managed to inject her words with an impressive amount of tetchiness. "But that's all it is. I have recently published my twentieth book, and I have killed at least one character in each of them. In my novel 'Eleven Ways to Die', there are just that; eleven murders, and each is quite different from any other. It is not surprising, therefore, that one of the deaths should resemble my father's."

I tried to put my thoughts in order before speaking again. "It's not just that both your father and a character in one of your books die in a strikingly similar fashion. From what I've been told, the story mirrors your life here rather closely."

She let out a girlish laugh, and I saw a glimpse of her more innocent side. "Oh, what a shame, Christopher; you haven't read it. I was hoping you had read my books." She turned her attention back to my grandfather. "And what about you, Lord Edgington? Are you an admirer?"

"I prefer the classics!" He succeeded in answering her but probably should have kept his mouth shut. His response made him sound quite childish.

"Then I will have to send you some of them. Perhaps I'll convert you yet."

"It's more than a coincidence," I declared, hoping that I was not too late to correct my previous approach. "In both your novel and real life, it is the father of the family who is pushed from the highest window of the house. You can dismiss it as happenstance, but a court may come to a different conclusion."

I was quite pleased with the decisive voice I'd used, but she did not seem particularly frightened by my hypothesis. She stared at the little boy holding a dolphin in the middle of the pond. It was not a real dolphin, of course, nor a real boy, but a bronze sculpture that was raised above the surface of the water on a small plinth.

"Very well." She smiled her scatter-brained smile, and I wondered what she had up her sleeve. "I will admit that it is more than just a coincidence if you'll be good enough to accept that there are at least three other suspects in my father's murder, and any one of them might be aware of the plot of my books."

"Eve and her husband appear to have an alibi. They were out of the house before seven o'clock when the police say your father was murdered." I only revealed this to see her reaction, and it was well worth the effort.

"Oh, I see…" She raised both eyebrows and frowned, as though impressed by her sister's story. What I couldn't tell was whether she actually believed it.

"Do your sisters read detective fiction?" A glimmer of Grandfather's confidence had returned to him.

"I very much doubt it. Though they like nothing more than reading my reviews in the paper. Well, the bad ones, at least. It's something of a contest between us. Some people are competitive at parlour games or tennis matches. We like to score points in the national press."

"Would that be one of the reasons you don't get on particularly well?" I had expected to turn over my duties to my grandfather, but new questions kept occurring to me.

"It's hard to say." She looked up at the sky rather curiously. I couldn't tell whether she was considering my question or checking for rain. "I suppose you must be right. Nessa is such a traditional sort. I think she believes that she was born into the wrong family, and that someone should write a royal biography of her. And as for her relationship with our father…"

When she didn't finish her sentence, I expected my grandfather to keep prying. Instead, he changed the subject. "What about Eve?"

Livia closed her eyes as if she'd had enough of the conversation. "Do you really need me to tell you? You saw what she was like last night. You endured the seven-hour tour and were party to her dinner conversation. Why Bertie ever married her is the real mystery of our family."

"So we've established that you don't think too highly of your sisters."

"Really, Lord Edgington, I think you can do better than that. It is not a question of the esteem in which I hold them. There are few people on this earth I prize more highly. But that does not mean I can tolerate them."

"So then, what of your father?" I had been holding my tongue for a good few seconds but decided to bring the conversation back to the murder itself. "I saw you looking out of your window just after he was found. You could summon no emotion at the sight of the poor man's broken body. It was almost as if you were glad he was dead."

"Oh, nonsense, boy!" She sounded rather like my grandfather just then and clearly wasn't intimidated by what I considered a vital point. "Just because I wasn't in floods of tears like Nessa and Eve, that doesn't mean I wanted the old chap to die."

"Very well, but you still haven't explained why you didn't love him." I could have said more but felt this was enough to make my point.

Her cold stare caught hold of me. "Can you honestly say that *your* father is perfect? In my experience, very few are the gentle bears we wish them to be. Mine was more like an old grizzly."

I was about to do as she'd suggested and consider how I really felt about my own dear Daddy – an act that was perhaps overdue – when she spoke again. "I stopped loving my father when I was eleven years old. I had come to realise that his reason for educating his daughters was not for our sense of fulfilment, but his own. We were a circus act that he would wheel out whenever his friends came to dinner. We were a music hall troupe for the rabble to adore. Not liberated, educated women, as he would always claim, but three exhibits in a museum of curiosities."

For the first time since we'd met, a vein of anger rose up from within her. Even when batting away my insistent questions, she had maintained the harmony in her singsong voice. And now she had finally shown what lay beneath her simple façade.

To my genuine surprise, it was at this moment that my vociferous partner decided to tread more softly. "I'm sorry to hear that you feel that way. I know what it's like to only be of interest to one's parents when there is an audience. My own mother and father were far from effusive when it came to their affection. They delegated most of their parental duties to my governess."

This was not the first time I had heard him speak of his childhood in such terms, but the emotion he shared with this practical stranger was far from expected.

He continued in the same mournful voice. "You know, I'll look rather foolish if I have to tell the young whippersnapper of a detective back at the house that I haven't been able to solve the case." He gazed at his reflection in the pond for a moment. On the far side, I noticed an orchard of trees that were laden with large, ripe apples, just waiting to be picked by a gardener or gobbled up by the birds. Turning back to us, there was a sad smile on his face as he made a plea. "So will you help us? As such a distinguished detective novelist, I rather think you must have some idea who wanted your father dead, or at least an explanation for why it might have occurred."

She observed him ever so sympathetically, then exploded with laughter. It was a high, gleeful sound which appeared to overwhelm her. "Oh, dear, Lord Edgington. You'll have to do better than that." Her amusement overwhelmed her once more, and she fought to control herself. A tiny sparkle of moisture appeared in her eyes, but she would not give into fully fledged tears. "Perhaps you should leave the theatrics to your charming grandson. I don't believe it is your forte."

Grandfather threw his arms in the air. I had always expected him to meet his match one day, and it appeared as though that day had now arrived. "I'll have you know that I'm much admired for my abilities at interviewing witnesses. Experts have written whole pamphlets on the very techniques you have seen at work here. Any failure you may have detected can only be down to the fact that… that… well, I'm not myself today, as anyone can see."

He crossed his arms and looked away again. It was hard to know what my duties were. On the one hand, we had a murder to solve and a witness to battle but, on the other, I felt a responsibility to my grandfather to make sure he wasn't too gloomy.

"You know, he really is a very good interviewer," I felt obliged to say before we could continue. "Such shifts in mood and approach normally leave our suspects quite wrongfooted."

He brightened just a touch and nodded to show his agreement. "Thank you, Christopher."

"That's right." I smiled in his direction. "My grandfather is an incredible detective. It simply isn't his fault that you've outwitted him."

"Christopher!" The horror on his face was beyond description and so I won't even try. All I can say is that any hope I might have fostered of embarking on a European tour with the old chap was now swiftly extinguished.

Luckily, Livia spoke again and helped put things right. "You are correct in one respect. As a literary assassin myself, I have given my father's murder some thought. I do not know who the killer is, though I am sure of one thing." Perhaps in keeping with the demands of her profession, she made us wait for a few more seconds before revealing her secret. It certainly added to the tension. "Whatever Eve told you wasn't true. I saw her depart on her walk this morning; the clock had just struck a quarter past seven."

CHAPTER TWELVE

"This changes everything!" I declared once the dear old novelist had toddled off back to the house, her long skirt trailing after her like a duck's tail.

"And why do you say that?" Grandfather was back to his imperious best. Without anyone around to challenge his brilliance – I definitely wasn't the man for that job – he was energised and self-assured. "Why should we trust the word of one sister over another?"

"Because…" It was my turn to lose my way. "Well… because Livia is a far more sympathetic character, and Eve is something of a harridan."

He frowned most melodramatically. "I will overlook your use of such offensive language and concentrate on the more pressing issue. You appear to have committed the very same error for which you recently criticised me. Are you now saying that we *should* judge a suspect's innocence based on her superficial demeanour?"

"Yes!" His dancing facial expressions soon taught me that this was the wrong answer and so I changed it. "By which I mean, no?"

"Exactly." He clapped his hands together and went for a stroll towards the pond before doubling back all the faster. "You are exactly right, Christopher. The answer is both yes and no at the very same time."

"I'm afraid I don't follow your meaning, Grandfather. Was Livia lying or telling the truth?"

He stopped moving for the briefest of moments and provided an answer that was just as confusing as anything else I'd heard that day. "Yes, she was." He changed direction a third time in quick succession and charted a course to Pearson House. He didn't appear to notice that I had not kept pace with him. Instead, he chattered away to himself, and I did my best to catch up. "If Livia is telling the truth, then Eve is lying. But if Eve is lying, then Livia might yet be lying as well. Two wrongs do not always make a right, and two lies offer no guarantee of the truth."

I didn't attempt to make sense of his gibberish. I was too busy cursing my luck for having to run so fast. I long for the day when one of our investigations does not require me to complete a short marathon or two.

"So where are we going in such a hurry?" I managed to pant out once I'd drawn alongside the athletic old chap.

"We are going nowhere in particular. I sometimes find that physical exercise helps me unlock the facts of a case and, as we speak, a picture is forming in my head." Such behaviour was eccentric even by his high standards.

"So, what do we do next?"

He didn't answer this question as we were interrupted by the sound of an argument which floated over to us from the house.

"I did it to protect you!" a male voice said. I don't know why I'm being so mysterious; there was only one man living in the grand old house. Assuming the police weren't in the music room making trouble, it obviously belonged to Bertie.

"You made everything worse," his wife replied in a growl. "If you'd held your tongue, we wouldn't be in this mess."

"I'm sorry, my darling. I really am, I just thought—"

"You didn't think. That's your problem, Bertie. You always—" Eve did not finish this sentence as my grandfather had rushed into the room.

"You!" he said with great authority. It was not until I followed him that I could see whom he had addressed. "Bertie, I wish to speak to you alone."

I know it's a saying that people turn as white as a sheet, but I'd rarely seen the transformation before my eyes. The blood drained from the man's face, and he stared at his wife as though pleading with her to make things right.

It was hard to know what Eve made of the situation. She looked both terrified of what Bertie might say to the deputised officer in charge of the case, and relieved not to have to talk to my grandfather again herself. Her husband opened his mouth and would have projected one of his characteristic laughs in our direction, but he simply didn't have the heart. He collapsed into an armchair, and Eve scuttled from the room.

Instead of instantly starting his questions, Grandfather made the man quake a while longer. He inspected the harpsichord and the selection of lutes and, just when it seemed the interview would never begin, he spun on the spot and shot four words across the room like a barrage of cannon balls. "Why did you lie?"

"I…" After the effort expended producing this simple reply, Bertie froze entirely.

"Livia saw Eve from her window as she set out for her walk. It was after the time the police estimate that Royston was murdered."

His throat dry, he coughed a little and responded in a nervous croak. "They can't possibly know with any certainty."

Grandfather had his response prepared and took three quick steps across the room to deliver it. "Perhaps not, but I can."

The time of five minutes past seven echoed in my head, although I was unsure how he could be so precise.

"I don't think I should be speaking to you." Any confidence that Bertie might have possessed had deserted him. He held onto his chair as though it were a life-buoy in a stormy sea.

"Tell me why you lied! You said that the two of you departed for your walk at half-past six, but I know that isn't true. So tell me what really happened."

"I…" Bertie was shaking.

I could only imagine the pressure that our suspects felt when peering into my grandfather's fierce visage at such a key moment in an investigation. It always made me glad that I was his assistant.

"Go on, tell me the truth. When did you decide to invent a story for Eve? And how did she react when you told her to go along with your plan?"

"There was no lie," he said with a sudden, fierce shudder, as though a cold wave had passed over him. "Perhaps Livia was mistaken. Perhaps she saw one of the household staff and mistook the maid for—"

"Her sister? No, I don't believe so. Livia was confident of what she saw. So why did you do it? Why did you lie?"

"I told you; it's the truth. You've no reason to believe her word over mine."

Grandfather was now the more ebullient of the two and let out a note of unimpressed laughter. "I might not have done if you were not now sitting before me looking as though the world were about to implode. If you had nothing to hide, you wouldn't be so frightened."

"I didn't lie. I really didn't. I just changed the particulars of our morning a fraction, and then—"

"You have just provided me with a really quite excellent definition of lying. Now, if you can explain why you felt the need to do so, maybe I'll soften my tone."

Bertie looked around the room in search of something or someone who could save him from the pit that he'd dug for himself. "I don't know why you think that I'm involved in any of this. I'm barely a member of the family. They certainly don't treat me like one. I'm just a bystander who happened to get swept along by their drama."

This was one excuse too many, and Grandfather had heard enough. "For goodness' sake, man. I'm not asking for proof of your moral fibre, and I don't want to hear your life story. All I wish to know is why you claimed to have left the house at six-thirty, when you didn't depart until three quarters of an hour later."

He had a look in his eyes which told us all we needed to know. It was fear I saw there: true fear. He glanced back at the door through which his wife had just left and uttered the words that we had gone there to hear. "I did it because I knew you would suspect Eve of murdering her father. I did it to protect her."

CHAPTER THIRTEEN

Everything happened so fast that there was barely time to examine the evidence and pick a likely suspect of my own. All the hard work had been done for me by this stage, and it would have seemed a little lazy to pick Eve, so after a quick review of the facts of the case, I decided on the Pearson House cook.

Admittedly, I didn't know her name, and we hadn't taken the time to interview her, but that just made her cunning all the more impressive. I couldn't put my finger on a motive, and I didn't know how she could have left the kitchen at a time when she was no doubt busy with her morning duties, but I felt fairly confident that it was– Oh, very well! Eve was the killer. Grandfather had more or less proven it, and I felt as stupid as ever not to have noticed all the signs pointing in her direction.

Though, now that I thought about it, I did find her a suspicious sort from the beginning. And though I'd largely stuck to Livia as my main suspect, in some ways, I was ahead of the legendary Lord Edgington! As Grandfather gave instructions to Bertie to seek out the other members of the family and bring them to the spot where Royston had died, it dawned on me that I had never fully trusted our culprit. Eve was a cold-hearted, money hungry murderess who had slain her own father to make up for a deficit in her bank account. And whilst I had no solid evidence on her other than the fact that her own husband had identified her as the murderer and lied to save her from gaol, I felt vindicated to have finally been right in my intuition... more or less.

"Christopher, we'll be home in time for afternoon tea." If Grandfather hadn't presented me with this piece of joyous news, I might very well have told him of my success.

"Excellent. Is there anything I can do to facilitate our departure?"

"Yes. While I have a word with Detective Inspector Tabert, perhaps you could find Delilah? She got excited and ran off somewhere, but I'm sure she'd hate to miss out on the big finish."

We both indulged in a smile then, and I went to fetch our dear pup from the meadow at the far border of the property. When we returned to the rear of the house, there was no sign of Grandfather, but D.I. Tabert and the rest of the family were in place on the terrace.

"Christopher?" Nessa began, when we'd been standing there in awkward silence for a short time. "Do you know why—"

She was interrupted by the sudden and quite alarming sight of my grandfather lurching around the corner of the house, making a noise like a tortured ghost.

"Eh-uh-haaaa," it went, and I assumed he was trying to unnerve our suspects. As I believe I have already expressed, he really did take things to extremes that weekend.

"You scared us half to death," I complained.

"I'm sorry." To be fair, he did sound a little remorseful. "I didn't mean to make such an unsettling sound. I think I must have swallowed a fly."

"More of your silly games, Edgington," Livia replied, already getting under the old chap's skin. "Isn't it about time you displayed some professionalism?"

He would not be drawn into another battle of wits – perhaps for fear he might lose – but grinned at her retort and addressed the reason we were gathered there. "I have asked you to come here, as I believe I can finally prove who murdered your father and father-in-law." He was quite the stickler for accuracy in his statements and pointed to the sisters and Bertie in turn.

"I know what you're going to say, and so I'll spare you the trouble." Eve was antagonistic from the first moment, but Grandfather raised one hand to silence her. To my surprise, she complied.

He cleared his throat and began his summary of the facts. "Royston Shipley was not born a wealthy man, but he strove to provide a good life for his children and succeeded in his plans. Pearson House is the culmination of his life's work; a grand monument to the efforts he made and his love for his family. My companions and I travelled all the way from Surrey, in large part to see the famous dwelling. And so, in a very real way, we came here to celebrate Mr Shipley's achievements."

"I know how this part of the story goes," Livia interrupted once more, and so my grandfather merely turned his back to her. "The detective lists all the evidence he's found before finally revealing the name of the killer after making us think it was six other people the whole time. I'm afraid you'll have to do more than that to impress me."

"Royston Shipley," he continued as though she hadn't spoken, "taught his daughters that they are the equals of any man, and that they deserve the very same opportunities. Whatever else may have motivated him, this fact deserves recognition, and I'm proud to have known him for the short time that I did."

Nessa nodded appreciatively. I wondered if she was the only one there who liked and perhaps even missed their deceased father.

"The question of who killed him has plagued me for ..." He stopped to look at his pocket watch. "... approximately the last three hours. With help from my colleagues in the police, I ruled out the Pearson House staff as suspects. Not only is there nothing to suggest that they would benefit from the murder, it is also obvious that, in his dotage, Royston was a popular master who will be missed. What this means, of course, is that the dead man was murdered by a member of his own family."

Standing in a semi-circle around my grandfather, his audience had fallen silent in anticipation of the name he would finally pronounce.

"As is typical during any murder investigation, I interviewed each suspect before coming to the right conclusion." Fine, he wouldn't say it immediately, but the killer's identity would not remain a secret for very much longer.

"You tell us the conclusion, and we'll decide whether you were right." The novelist sounded ruder with each intervention. This was another side to her personality that we hadn't seen before, and I wondered which was the real Livia Shipley.

With the disruption over, Grandfather wore a carefree expression and continued with his tale. "I kept an open mind and considered your guilt one by one. Livia and Eve appeared to be the obvious culprits, not that their spiky personalities, when compared with their warm-hearted sister's, would count as evidence in court. And in fact, I witnessed a fire inside Nessa this weekend, and I couldn't overlook the rivalry she shared with her younger sibling, nor the complicated relationship that she clearly had with her father."

Nessa straightened her back and looked down at the space where her father's body had been found. "I doubt I'm the only person who has felt underappreciated by a parent." Her voice was as fragile as a frozen lake in springtime. "Nothing I did was ever quite enough for my father, but that doesn't mean I killed him. If anything, I have to live with the knowledge that any chance I might have had to impress him has passed."

She looked around her family in the hope that one of them might comfort her but, for the second time that day, that task fell to my grandfather. "I am sorry to hear that, Nessa. But through our interactions, I came to see that the sorrow you have shown is genuine. I have found no evidence to prove that you murdered your father, so I turned my attention to your sisters."

He split his gaze between the remaining suspects, who were arranged in a semi-circle to observe the final part of his spectacle.

"Livia, in particular, gave me reason to believe she could be the killer when she openly confessed that she felt no emotion for her father." He stepped closer at this point to stand in front of the author. "I have met countless murderers who feel nothing for their victims, but even more importantly, Royston Shipley's death was a near copy of one of the characters in Livia's novel 'Eleven Ways to Die'."

It was fascinating to see these two contrasting titans of detection – one within the realms of fiction and the other in real life – clash against one another like dinosaurs of old. I felt that Grandfather was hoping to land a decisive blow with this comment, but the second Shipley girl was resilient and merely raised her eyebrows.

"According to her sisters, Livia had always had morbid interests. And yet, such simplistic judgements cannot be considered evidence of a person's guilt. Not every novelist who writes of murder should automatically be considered a murderer, and I could not eliminate the possibility that the killer copied the method for the victim's murder from Livia's book. So, with nothing to say she was the culprit, I moved on to the youngest of the Shipley siblings." I believe that Grandfather may have winked at Livia just then. It was hard to tell whether it was a taunt or an acknowledgement of her innocence, but it certainly surprised her.

"A lesser detective might have singled Eve out from the beginning for her abrasive manner, but I gave her the benefit of the doubt. It takes every sort of person to weave our human tapestry, and it was not until she brought up the topic of murder at dinner that I found anything particularly unusual about her."

Eve was the only one there who had remained silent throughout

Lord Edgington's speech. Even now, she barely moved a muscle, as a strong wind blew her wispy grey hair across her face. "She is not the first person I have known who wished to discuss the viability of a perfect crime, but her interest seemed more than merely academic. And that is why, when her father's body was discovered here this morning, my mind went back to last night's discussion."

Grandfather had increased his pace a little and drew out certain words in each sentence as if his meaning should be clear to all. "If Royston had been shot or stabbed, I might not have lent this fact such importance, but that is not how he died. The poor man fell to his death, and we know it was no accident as his nurse assured Detective Inspector Tabert that his window was closed when she had checked on him the previous night. Furthermore, the fact his hands were at his side when the body was discovered would suggest that he was unconscious as he hit the ground. Considering the strength of the medicine I found on his night table, it would not have been difficult for the killer to remove him from bed and push him through the recently opened window."

He came to a sudden stop and peered into the face of each person there. I didn't know what to think when he looked at me. I was half terrified that he suspected my involvement in the killing. That would certainly have been an unexpected conclusion.

"Not quite the perfect crime, then, but close enough to the template I had laid out for you all. The template that Eve had requested." Doubling back on his path (for approximately the seventh time that day) Grandfather placed himself before our inevitable culprit. "It was you, was it not, who insisted that I should devise an unsolvable murder?"

She said nothing.

"You are also the only sister whose success as a writer has suffered since an ill-advised publication diminished your reputation. The only one who wishes to embark on an expensive voyage to South America to prepare for another book." A look of mock surprise crossed his features. "I imagine that your inheritance would help you pay your way."

Eve remained silent, but I'm sure a doctor with a good stethoscope would have heard her bones quietly trembling.

"The only sister whose husband invented an alibi on her behalf because even he was convinced that you were capable of such violence."

"It's not true." His laughter long forgotten, Bertie's statement emerged as a tortured squeal.

"But it really isn't," Eve echoed. "I didn't kill Daddy, I would never—"

This wasn't Lord Edgington's first or even his fifty-first time staring into a killer's eyes, and he was too quick for her. "But you do admit that you are in dire straits financially, and that you lied about the time at which you left the house this morning?"

It was no longer a matter of choice or obstinacy; she had no idea how to answer him, and so he pressed on with the case against her.

"Your husband lied for you, and you went along with his plan. He could see no hope after you asked me to help you plan a murder in front of your whole family. He invented a story that was undone by your sister Livia, who happened to look out of her window this morning when you were leaving the house, some ten minutes after your father was already dead."

"This isn't right." It was Eve's turn to wail. It was almost enough to make me feel sorry for her... almost.

"And yet you haven't denied one single part of my story. The facts are plain for all to see. You killed your father in order to receive your inheritance and then lied about where you were at the time of the murder. Am I missing anything?"

Her eyes jumped from one sister to the other, before coming to a rest on her husband. She reached out to him with one limp hand, but there was nothing he could do to save her.

"Tell me, Eve," my grandfather demanded one last time. "You're a writer; tell me what's missing from this story."

Tears rolled down her sharp cheeks before cascading towards the paving slabs. As the inspector fished into his pocket for his handcuffs, knots formed in my throat and stomach at the same time. The wretched creature would spend the rest of her life in prison simply because she–

"It was him," Livia said, to interrupt my really quite poetic thoughts. Her hand shot out in front of her, and the words ignited the scene. "It was Bertie, not Eve. He killed our father."

CHAPTER FOURTEEN

Before anyone could say another word, D.I. Tabert jumped forward to nab his man. Bertie was too quick and pushed the skinny officer away to dash off through the flowerbeds to a place of relative safety.

"Eve, my darling, nothing is how it seems." His voice was suddenly desperate. "I swear things are not as black as they might look."

"You lied, man." Lord Edgington had not finished his explanation after all, though he did sound a little miffed that Livia had spoilt his big finale. "Not for your wife, but for yourself. You convinced her that everyone would think her the killer, when in reality, you were the one in need of an alibi.

"Bertie Peregrine, a man who everyone adored. A land agent whose business was failing and who, by murdering his father-in-law, could gain the chance to sell this famous property thanks to the will that would allow any of his heirs to dissolve the estate. You would have convinced Eve to sell her family home just as you convinced her to go along with your lie."

To be perfectly honest, I'd forgotten this significant detail. Luckily, my grandfather hadn't.

Bertie wasn't giving up and stretched his hands out in desperation as he spoke. "I did this for you, Evie. I knew we didn't have the money for the trip to South America. But if you didn't travel, you couldn't write another book." His expression was one of pure torment as he repeated his sad refrain. "I did this for you."

Grandfather was tired of his excuses and talked over him. "As I investigated the possibility that one of the three sisters was responsible for the killing, I never lost sight of the second and most important part of my plan for a perfect crime. It is not enough to make a murder look like an accident or suicide. You must also ensure that, should anyone suspect foul play, there is a likely suspect to take the blame. My grandson, Christopher, assumed that was your wife for the simple reason that she was not the cheeriest host when we arrived. But you knew better."

Livia inhaled a loud breath just then and stepped forward to heap more guilt on him. "You thought that I would make a good scapegoat?" She allowed herself a disbelieving gasp before continuing. "You are the only person in the family who has read my books, and you knew that, with a little bit of investigating, the police would suspect me. Poor, sad Livia with her unladylike obsessions. Pathetic Livia, the queer fish of the family, whose only love is the macabre fiction she writes. You deceitful swine, Bertie."

It was at this point that she went charging after him. I have no doubt she would have given him a good socking if the diversion hadn't allowed D.I. Tabert to sneak up on the fearful chap from the other side of the flowerbed and lay his hands on the man.

"Arrest me. Lock me up," he screamed as she landed a glancing blow. "Just keep me away from that woman!"

"How dare you use my books against me?" At this, she picked up a handful of earth and hurled it in his direction. It was the last missile she would throw as, seeing the risk to D.I. Tabert, Grandfather stepped in to stay her arm.

"Very good, Livia. Bertie will get the punishment he deserves; you should have no fear on that score."

Eve had fallen to her knees in despair and her big sister had gone to comfort her. The two women held the man they had trusted in their gaze, and it was hard to know what they felt as Livia pulled free from my grandfather and went chasing after the killer once more.

"How could you do such a thing?" she screamed, the rage flying from her mouth. "You inhuman brute. How could you kill another person?"

"You have to protect me from her," Bertie insisted as he hid behind the now grinning policeman. "She's entirely hysterical!"

"I'll show you just how hysterical I can be!" Livia had stolen Grandfather's cane and was leaning around D.I. Tabert to give Bertie a real thwacking.

"Don't you think you should you do something?" I felt compelled to ask my illustrious mentor, who was enjoying the spectacle as much as anyone else.

He stroked his long white beard and his face turned serious. "No. No, I do not."

CHAPTER FIFTEEN

After Bertie was escorted away – without any major injuries, I should add – it was time to pack our possessions and leave.

"Lord Edgington, it has been a pleasure doing battle with you," Livia announced at the front door where she had been waiting for us. "I'm just sorry it had to be under such difficult circumstances."

"A pleasure indeed." Grandfather looked at her as though appraising the part she had played. "I must confess that your conclusions on the case were most astute. I have met many great detectives in my life, but few who could solve a perfect crime."

She flinched at these words, and I think she finally realised that he was not chastising but complimenting her. She blinked a few times – presumably to confirm that she was not dreaming or concussed – and then delivered a curious response.

"That's good of you to say. Though I've often thought that, if I hadn't taken up writing detective fiction, I might well have devoted my talents to a less respectable profession."

Like a general examining a fellow soldier, Grandfather nodded sternly. "Oh, absolutely. I have no doubt that we would both make the most fantastic criminals. Though I feel that murder would be somewhat beneath us, even then."

Livia let out a muffled laugh and extended her hand to the legend in our midst. "Perhaps we'll get the chance to work together again one day."

"Yes, I believe I'd like that." He shook her hand, and the pair smiled at one another while our dog, Delilah, ran exultant laps up and down the length of the drive. "It would give me the opportunity to show you just how capable an interviewer I normally am."

She smiled appreciatively at him, then turned to head into the house.

I was proud and simultaneously a little jealous of them both. I was used to the fact that, for every small success I had when investigating such cases, I took two large jumps backwards. And yet I really should have considered Bertie as a likely suspect. On the bright side, I'd spotted a lovely bakery on the drive through Suffolk and hoped Grandfather would let us stop for some scones on the way home. What in life cannot be remedied with a few delicious cakes?

Todd had already put our bags into the car and, as I had finally changed out of my nightwear, which I hadn't had the opportunity to remove all morning, it was time to go home.

"Grandfather, there is one thing I don't understand," I told him as we crunched our way across the gravel towards his navy-blue Rolls Royce.

"Oh, yes, what's that?"

I thought for a moment and realised that my statement wasn't quite true. "Well, in actual fact, there's something I do understand – but feel I ought to check. It was the pipes, wasn't it?"

"I beg your pardon?"

"The noisy pipes in the house meant no one heard poor Royston crashing to the earth from the top floor. All Bertie had to do was to turn the taps on and the sound carried throughout the building. The nurse thought nothing of it as she'd grown accustomed to the noise."

"That's precisely it, Christopher. Excellent work."

This was some consolation for the fact I had, yet again, failed to identify the killer. And I had more still to reveal. "That was how you knew the time of death, wasn't it? At five minutes past seven, Bertie walked his sedated and sleeping father-in-law from his bed and pushed him from the window."

"Wonderful, my boy. That's truly exceptional reasoning. Is there anything else that you initially found confusing but were finally able to deduce?"

His warm tone filled me with confidence. "Yes, I believe there was. You see, I couldn't comprehend why anyone would have committed a murder with the great Lord Edgington on the premises." For once, I made him wait in suspense. "But Bertie must have wanted you here to unearth the evidence against Livia. He underestimated you, of course, and I suspect that he wasn't as clever as he wished to believe."

He pulled his neck in to look at me from a new angle over the bonnet of the Rolls. "That's an extremely perceptive judgement, my boy." I think he was rather impressed. "Perhaps your first lesson should be to speak up when you have a good idea from now on."

"Isn't that my second lesson?"

"Is it?" He looked at the multicoloured trees overhead and

considered the possibility. "You know I've quite lost count already, but it's a lesson, nonetheless. Lesson number one, two, or perhaps even three: make sure that you tell me what you're thinking when I'm too busy to notice."

Todd had finished cranking the engine and ran around the car to open the door for his master. "Straight home is it, M'Lord?"

"Yes, I don't see why—"

"Grandfather!" I yelled before he could say anything else. "I'm taking your advice and have decided to tell you what I'm thinking. I think we should stop off in Darsham for some scones."

He surveyed me in that wise old way of his before delivering his verdict. "That is a wonderful idea, my boy. I should have thought of it myself."

We climbed aboard, only for Delilah to come shooting around the outside of the house with her tail wagging. She let out a few reproachful barks and jumped onto my lap.

"No, of course we didn't forget you," her owner insisted. "You have a terribly suspicious nature, Delilah. You should be more trusting."

As the two conducted this really quite ridiculous conversation, and Todd pulled off along the drive, I spotted a face watching us from one of the upper-floor windows. It was hard to say whether it was that supremely talented mystery writer Livia Shipley, or a ghost called Martin, but I knew which I thought more likely.

The End (For Now...)

READ MORE LORD EDGINGTON MYSTERIES TODAY...

- **Murder at the Spring Ball**
- **Death From High Places** (free e-novella available exclusively at benedictbrown.net. Paperback and audiobook are available at Amazon)
- **A Body at a Boarding School**
- **Death on a Summer's Day**
- **The Mystery of Mistletoe Hall**
- **The Tangled Treasure Trail**
- **The Curious Case of the Templeton-Swifts**
- **The Crimes of Clearwell Castle**
- **A Novel Way to Kill**
- **The Snows of Weston Moor**
- **What the Vicar Saw**
- **Blood on the Banister**
- **A Killer in the Wings**
- **The Christmas Bell Mystery**
- **The Puzzle of Parham House** (Spring 2024)

Check out the complete Lord Edgington Collection at Amazon

The first nine Lord Edgington audiobooks, narrated by the actor George Blagden, are available now on all major audiobook platforms. There will be more coming soon.

ABOUT THIS BOOK

Much of the inspiration for this book came through an unexpected stroke of luck. My family and I go on holiday to a cottage in Suffolk every year to attend a music festival, and I noticed that, just along the road from where we stay, there was a rather beautiful manor house. I tried to find out who lived there and ended up getting in touch with the owners and asking whether they'd allow me to use a photo of the house on the front of the book. They said they didn't mind as long as it would not lead to an influx of people storming their gates.

It's very hard to find good quality, legally licensed photos of such properties, so that was the first achievement, but the house I then visited and photographed happened to be full of amazing stories that would go on to influence this book.

In the nineteenth century, the manor housed a family with five daughters, four of whom would go on to become incredibly successful writers. Many of the details of the Shipleys from this book were taken from that real literary family. Their father took special care with his daughters' education, and almost bankrupted the family through the upkeep of the immense house. Much like the Brontës, the daughters became famous and respected and there was a historian and a travel writer among them – though I added the mystery novelist to fit with the plot I had planned. Oh, and the murder never happened, of course. The real house has all sorts of links to famous figures from history, including Isaac Newton – not his cousin or gardener, as in the Shipleys' case. The house, apparently, even had a ghost called Martin, which was too perfect not to mention in the story.

This is the first book which I have written whilst staying in a suitably ancient building. I was on holiday near Verona in an eighteenth-century farmhouse in the hills overlooking the city. This did not greatly inspire my plot, but the outdated plumbing did give me the idea for the noisy pipes in Pearson House.

Most of my books have a song in somewhere and "Oh! Mr Porter" is a British music hall staple written in 1892 by George and Thomas Le

Brunn. It's a song about a woman who gets on the wrong train, and I'm sure it would have had audiences rolling in the aisles. It even got a mention in James Joyce's "Ulysses", which was published four years before this book is set.

"A NOVEL WAY TO KILL" COCKTAIL

In each of the "Lord Edgington Investigates…" books there is a cocktail curated by our very own cocktail expert Francois Monti. This time around, I asked him for a drink that an eighteen-year-old boy definitely wouldn't enjoy, and Sazerac fit the bill. It is one of the oldest American cocktails – some say the oldest. Dating from the 1850s, the ingredients have changed several times over the decades. The absinthe has been exchanged for other anis-based drinks – as absinthe was banned in America for over a century – and the cognac was briefly replaced with rye when European crops faced the phylloxera epidemic.

I don't normally like strong alcohol, but I am partial to absinthe after the heady days when I first moved to Barcelona. Several memorable nights out started (and several forgotten nights finished) at Bar Marsella. The bar, which opened in 1820, is famous for a similar drink to Sazerac – with an absinthe-dowsed sugar cube being set on fire and then drowned in water. The bar made it into a Woody Allen film and played host to Picasso and Hemingway among others. I'm pretty sure that the cobwebs on the bottles around the bar are almost as old too.

The classic Sazerac recipe is…

5 cl cognac
1 cl absinthe
One sugar cube
Two dashes Peychaud's Bitters

But the real joy is in the way it is prepared with two chilled glasses. The absinthe is used to wash and flavour the first glass and the other ingredients are mixed in the second before being stirred with ice and then strained into the original receptacle. It's strong stuff, but you only live once.

The idea for our cocktail pages was inspired by my friend and the "Lord Edgington Investigates…" official cocktail expert, Francois Monti. You can get his brilliant book "101 Cocktails to Try Before you Die" at Amazon.

ABOUT ME

Writing has always been my passion. It was my favourite half-an-hour a week at primary school, and I started on my first, truly abysmal book as a teenager. So it wasn't a difficult decision to study literature at university which led to a master's in creative writing.

I'm a Welsh-Irish-Englishman originally from **South London** but now living with my French/Spanish wife and presumably quite confused infant daughter in **Burgos**, a beautiful mediaeval city in the north of Spain. I write overlooking the Castilian countryside, trying not to be distracted by the vultures, hawks and red kites that fly past my window each day.

When Covid 19 hit in 2020, the language school where I worked as an English teacher closed down and I became a full-time writer. I have two murder mystery series. There are already six books written in **"The Izzy Palmer Mysteries"** which is a more modern, zany take on the genre. I will continue to alternate releases between Izzy and Lord Edgington. I hope to release at least ten books in each series.

I previously spent years focussing on kids' books and wrote everything from fairy tales to environmental dystopian fantasies, right through to issue-based teen fiction. My book **"The Princess and The Peach"** was long-listed for the Chicken House prize in The Times and an American producer even talked about adapting it into a film. I'll be slowly publishing those books over the next year whenever we find the time.

"A Novel Way to Kill" is the ninth title in the "Lord Edgington Investigates…" series. The next book will be out in the winter and there's another novella available free if you sign up to my **readers' club.** If you feel like telling me what you think about Chrissy and his grandfather, my writing or the world at large, I'd love to hear from you, so feel free to get in touch via…

www.benedictbrown.net

Printed in Great Britain
by Amazon

40345905R00057